THROUGH A LENS

A FLORENTINE ROMANCE

JERILYN MCINTYRE

Copyright © 2024 by Jerilyn McIntyre

Published by Flock Publishing, a division of Pink Flamingo Productions

All rights reserved.

No part of this book may be reproduced in any form or by any electronic or mechanical means, including information storage

and retrieval systems, without written permission from the author, except for the use of brief quotations in a book review

Proofreading by Paige Editorial Services

Design by MiblArt

Formatting by Jenn D. Young

✯ Created with Vellum

Give me grace, my Lord, be lenient with me, In your kindness give me the courage
To write the story that I hold clasped in my mind....

—*Lucrezia Tornabuoni de' Medici*

For David. The perfect partner.

THANK YOU

To fellow writers Sylvia Torti and members of my writing group (Joan Coles, Klancy de Nevers, Donna Graves, Karen Hayes, Debbie Leaman, and Elizabeth Mitchell) for their thoughtful comments and suggestions on multiple earlier drafts of this novel, and to David Smith, business partner and spouse extraordinaire, for applying his considerable skills as a writer and editor to preparation of the manuscript. In loving memory of my parents, Maxine and Frank McIntyre, and my brother Joel, who throughout my life encouraged and shaped my interest in writing and storytelling.

The cathedral was empty except for the two who knelt in prayer silently at the side altar. An early morning mass, as was their custom. Saints looked down from on high, denizens of the huge dome over the nave of the huge, echoing church. They saw. No one else did.

It was over in a moment. A flash of knives, a muffled shout, the sound of a scuffle, hands parrying thrusts that somehow still found their mark.

One lay dead, the other badly wounded. Soon the rest of the city would find out.

CHAPTER 1

Julia woke to the sound of church bells.

She raised her head from her pillow, rubbed her eyes, and looked around. The briefcase, camera bag, and clothing from her half-unpacked garment bag were strewn around a space she didn't recognize.

She sat up, stretched, and yawned. *I'm so tired. Where am I?*

Gradually everything came back to her: the long flight to Florence and the trip from the airport, her taxi careening through the narrow streets of the historic center of the city as the driver practiced his small talk on her. She wasn't very responsive. Her Italian was rusty—she hadn't used it since she was an exchange student in Florence ten years earlier—and she hadn't felt like talking. Arriving in the middle of the afternoon after having left Seattle the previous day, she was exhausted. The taxi deposited her at her destination, a boutique hotel tucked in a small piazza away from the noise and bustle of the tourists and traffic nearby.

The woman at the reception desk was brisk, polite, and efficient. *No small talk from her, thank God.*

Equipped with an outsized, ornately decorated key as well as directions to the farthest wing of the hotel, Julia found her way to her room, intending only to take a short nap and then get up in time for *cena* and an after-dinner exploration of her neighborhood. The morning light seeping through the shutters in her room told her she had slept much longer--but not well. Her transatlantic trip had left her weary. Fatigue gripped her so tightly her bones hurt.

She threw back the covers and rolled out of bed, shuffling to the shower where she let the cold-water spray wake her. Finally, dressed in tailored jacket, sweater, and wool slacks, casually but appropriately for fashion-conscious Florence, she felt ready for the breakfast buffet in the hotel dining room and for her later meeting with Robert.

By the middle of the morning, she was seated comfortably on a leather chair in the back corner of the lobby. She liked to be where she could enjoy her privacy while using her photographer's eye to study people walking by. It was out of the way and quiet too, a place where she could sit in silence, sip an espresso, and wait for her old friend.

CHAPTER 2

Robert checked his watch as he maneuvered his Fiat into the parking area at the side of the piazza in front of the hotel. *A little early. I shouldn't be so obvious about how happy I am to see her again.*

The long and complicated history of their relationship still hurt.

They had met in an art history class their first semester in college. On study dates and excursions to local museums, they found they shared a mutual love of Renaissance art. Robert became so enthralled with it that he decided to major in European cultural history, concentrating on medieval and Renaissance Italy. The time they spent together led to a brief affair—Julia's first sexual experience and Robert's only serious relationship to that point. It lasted throughout the spring and summer until she left in the fall for her sophomore study-abroad year in Florence. While there, she wrote to him that she had become seriously involved with Bill, a graduate student in architecture and design.

Her news was hard for Robert to accept at first. He sent

an angry reply, but when she returned from Europe, engaged, he became at least outwardly reconciled to his new role as friend and confidante. *What should I do?* he thought at the time. *Maybe they'll break up and she'll come back to me.*

That phase of their friendship continued until his graduation from college when he departed for his own trip to Italy—to travel and explore the country and its way of life for a year, he told her—promising to stay in touch with her while he was gone.

Eight years passed and their communications with each other became less frequent, although they kept up with important developments in their lives through Christmas cards and occasional letters. She wrote to him when her engagement to Bill ended, and he let her know that he was living in Florence, writing historical fiction while earning money on the side as a freelance journalist. Caught up in the demands of their respective careers, neither had married.

In recent months, as her current trip to Florence began to take shape, she wrote to him to ask if he would have time to meet with her. She wanted the help he could give on her upcoming magazine assignment. His response was warm. *Maybe she misses me. Maybe we can pick up where we left off.*

He came through the revolving doors of the hotel's entrance, looked in her direction, and waved. As he approached, Julia rose to greet him, struck by the changes in his appearance. His sandy-blonde hair, a bit long and unkempt when he was younger, was now trimmed into a crew cut. Leaner and more athletic than he had been in college, he walked across the lobby with a confident swagger.

"You owe me a big hug," he said. Laughing, she wrapped her arms around his waist and leaned forward to kiss him on the cheek. That wasn't the greeting he wanted. He pulled her close and pressed his lips to hers, hard. "That's for old times' sake," he said, still holding her tight.

She looked surprised. *Might be better to take it slow.* He backed off and tipped his head to get a good look at her. "She lives!" he said, grinning.

"Barely," she answered and, grabbing his hand, drew him to the corner of the lobby where she had been sitting. "Have a seat—and some coffee. I don't think the hotel will mind."

They settled into chairs facing each other. His smile changed to a look of concern.

"Are you okay?" he asked. "You're a little pale. Something happen on the way over?"

"No," she said. "I just didn't get a good night's sleep. Probably jet lag. You know me. I have trouble after overnight flights."

"Still?" He smiled. "I thought that was only when you were young. Didn't you just turn 30?"

"I'm not over the hill yet," she said, wagging her finger at him. "Thirty is the new twenty, hadn't you heard?"

They fell easily into the kind of banter they had always enjoyed with each other, teasing, reminiscing, and catching up with news about mutual friends. And then Robert became more serious.

"So what's up? What brings you to Florence?"

"I'm working on a piece for a travel magazine. About touring in the new millennium. But in my preparation for the piece, I discovered how important the Great Jubilee will be in Italy. Can you tell me more about that? It might provide an intriguing sidebar."

Her invitation was enough to swing him into gear. The Jubilee, he said, was the twenty-sixth of a series of Holy Years celebrated at intervals by the Roman Catholic Church. Beginning in the year 1300, they were occasions for pilgrims to return to Rome to seek reconciliation with God and to pray at certain sites holy to the faith.

"Jubilee 2000 is the first to coincide with the turning of a millennium," he explained. "Pope John Paul II has given it special emphasis. He sees it as an opportunity to unify the Christian family and reach out to other faiths."

It was also turning out to be an opportunity for renewal of a different sort. Robert described the financial support that was being offered in cities throughout the country to refurbish and renovate religious sites and other monuments that tourists might want to visit.

"By now, even though it's only spring, almost everything is finished. About twenty million visitors are expected to come for the Jubilee. What's interesting to me is that the locals are all very caught up in the historical significance of the event. Ties to other historical episodes are mentioned constantly in conversations I've had with friends here. The lessons of the past seem to be on people's minds."

As Robert talked, Julia was caught up in his excitement. Watching his eyes and animated gestures, she was struck as she had always been by his enthusiasm and his unflagging energy.

He brought her thoughts back to the task at hand. "You're staying in one of the most interesting sections of Florence," he said. "This is a tower neighborhood, and towers used to play a big role in community identification and neighborhood loyalties."

"I've read a little about them. They're medieval in origin, aren't they?"

"Most of them are. One of them was even a women's prison in the 1100s."

"For what kind of prisoners? For what kinds of crimes?"

"I'm not sure exactly," Robert replied. "I don't know why they needed a prison for them, but in many ways, Florentine society in that era was definitely not friendly to women."

"I wonder if anything like that is still going on? It might be an interesting angle for my article."

CHAPTER 3

The neighborhood around the hotel was one of the oldest in Florence. As a student, Julia loved exploring its cluster of historic sites. After she and Robert agreed to meet for dinner, she decided to use the rest of the day to become reacquainted with a city she had once known so well.

Leaving the piazza in front of her hotel, she was caught up in the brisk foot traffic along the adjoining street. She paused, backed up against the rough stone of an old tower house now transformed into a shoe store. When space on the narrow sidewalk opened, she headed toward the Uffizi gallery.

She looked forward to shopping on the Via dei Calzaiuoli along the way. In her earlier days in Florence, she had enjoyed haggling with the vendors who displayed their wares on carpets on the sides of the busy street. Their merchandise (sold without a license and the object of police patrols) was a colorful array of scarves, purses, and assorted leather goods designed to capture the interest of tourists and other customers interested in cheaper products and souvenirs. There were always bargains to be found.

But the bustling tourist scene she expected to find wasn't there. For a moment, she thought that the police had moved through the area, triggering a wild scramble as peddlers gathered up their wares and scampered away into surrounding neighborhoods so they couldn't be arrested. But this total absence of people, including tourists and other shoppers, was unusual.

Ducking into the open doorway of a *bar pasticceria,* she was greeted by the rich aroma of coffee and the hissing and thumping sound of an espresso machine. The *barista* was pulling shots for two women who were pointing at a selection of freshly baked pastries.

Julia approached the counter. Turning to the other customers, she asked, "What happened outside?"

"An attack in front of the Duomo," one of the women responded, her command of English seasoned by a Florentine accent. "The police blocked off the area when they arrived. Everybody hurried to get away from that part of the city. A woman we ran into when we were coming here said two men had been stabbed."

The woman's friend shook her head and sniffed in disapproval. "More bloodshed. It's getting to be common again, just like the Medici and the Pazzi."

Julia was startled. The woman's remark equated the stabbing with the 15th-century attempted assassination of Lorenzo the Magnificent by representatives of the Pazzi family.

"You're not serious, are you?" she said. "That was a very different era."

The woman shrugged. "A lot of violent stuff still goes on, and some of it is political," she said to Julia. "It always has been...." Her voice trailed off as she reached into her purse to pay for her food. With her friend, she then moved to a table at the back of the shop.

Julia ordered an espresso and selected a chocolate *cornetto* from a plate on the counter. She carried both to a place next to a window where she could watch for renewed activity on the street outside and think about what she had just heard.

The Medici-Pazzi attack was a well-known incident in the history of Florentine politics. Lorenzo Medici and his younger brother Giuliano had entered the Duomo for morning mass at the high altar. Agents of the Pazzi family, their wealthy political and economic rivals, attacked them, prompted by the Pazzi's desire to control the government of Florence. Lorenzo had escaped, but Giuliano had been mortally wounded, stabbed repeatedly by Pazzi partisans disguised as priests.

The location and the attack that morning had apparently evoked memories of the city's turbulent past. *That's incredible*, Julia thought, shaking her head. *But this must be what Robert was talking about this morning—the way people are finding historical connections to things that are happening now.* She tore a piece from her pastry and popped it into her mouth. *That's so like Florence*, she smiled. *The past and the present existing side by side.*

Shoppers and tourists gradually came into view again and the *pasticceria* began to fill with customers. Gathering up her purse, she left for the Piazza della Signoria, eager to spend her afternoon in Florence's most famous art collection,

. . .

"Thank Heavens for Robert," she muttered as she picked up her ticket at the will-call window, avoiding the long line for admission to the Uffizi. It wasn't the high season yet, but the approach of the millennium had brought an influx of tourists earlier than was typical. Robert warned her that the city's main attractions might be unusually crowded.

The galleries began on the third floor of the museum. A small elevator on the ground floor was available to transport visitors a few at a time, but she chose the stairway, a slower approach that gave her time for reflection. She felt excited anticipation at first and then intense emotions and memories of times when she had visited the museum with Bill, walking arm in arm with him up the long staircase.

They had met soon after her arrival in Florence. Three years older, he was there on a graduate fellowship. They fell in love as they spent more and more of their time together, exploring the city and the rest of Italy. By the end of the year, they were engaged.

That was such a long time ago.

As she studied the paintings of the ethereal medieval madonnas in the first room, an American tour group came along, clustered around a guide who began her brisk overview of the collections. Their delight as they encountered the treasures of the museum for the first time reinforced her own joy in seeing them again. She followed them into the next salons.

Botticelli's "Primavera" and "Birth of Venus" evoked a collective gasp of appreciation, followed by murmured grumbling. One of the women in the group spoke up. "What's with the shiny overlays?" she asked. Fiberglass shields covered the Botticelli masterpieces and other artwork in the galleries. In the bright light of the salons, they reflected the images of those who were looking at the paintings. It was admittedly distracting.

"The protection is necessary," the tour guide explained, "because of threats of vandalism and the need for security in art galleries throughout Italy."

"Well, it makes me dizzy," the woman complained. "I don't like to see my own image when I look at these paintings. Surely there was another way to protect them."

The guide stared at her for a moment and then shrugged. "It is a shame, isn't it," she said with an edge to her voice and pointed to the next salon. "I'll meet you there. That will give you a few minutes to enjoy this room by yourselves."

Julia decided to move on too, to other salons where there were more works she loved. She wanted to see them again, without the reminders of the violent modern world that kept intruding on her return to Florence.

By the end of the long afternoon, she was exhausted. Back at the hotel, she stopped at the small bar tucked to the side of the lobby. Robert would be coming later to pick her up for dinner. For now, she just wanted to sit quietly and sort through the feelings that had been awakened in her.

With a glass of *pinot grigio* in hand, she selected a table close to the warmth of the fireplace in the ancient tower around which the hotel's modern structure had been built. She kicked her shoes off, slumped into the cushions of the banquette lining the side of the room, and propped her feet on the seat of the chair opposite her, tipping her head back against the stone wall behind her. The bartender was busy washing dishes and straightening the tables turned askew by earlier customers. He left Julia alone, for which she was grateful. In this late afternoon, they were the only two in the bar.

A whirl of images spun through her mind, some from her student days, others from her childhood. Lost in her memories, she felt herself relaxing into a soft wine-induced reverie, slowly drifting asleep. She awakened suddenly to a sharp sound close to her. She sat up and looked around. The bartender was on the other side of the room, putting away glassware on shelves behind the bar. No one else was there.

She glanced to her side at the tower. She rubbed her eyes and looked closely at the fireplace. Nothing there.

Must have been my imagination.

Taking a deep breath to clear her head, she sank back into the cushions behind her, sipped her wine, and felt the emptiness in the room.

CHAPTER 4

As Robert had promised, "Paoli" was special. The food was an assortment of well-prepared Florentine specialties, but it was the ambiance that enchanted Julia. Set in the basement of an old building, its walls and especially its vaulted ceiling were adorned with bright, colorful frescoes, said to be medieval in origin. The clientele was also an assortment, a mix of native Florentine regulars and visitors from several foreign tour groups. Tonight, the majority of them seemed to be from Japan. Julia listened to the waiter switching from speaking Japanese, then English and Italian as he moved from one table to the next.

She thought again about how she and Robert had changed. When they first met, she had been attracted to his bookish obsessions as well as his boyish good looks. Over the years, maturity and experience had given his face some different aspects. A slightly furrowed brow, a few wrinkles around the mouth—laugh lines. Wire-rimmed glasses now magnified the blue eyes that looked out on the world with bemused curiosity.

Visually, they were a contrast, she with long, dark curls (unlike the short bob she had worn in college) and Robert now with his close-cropped blonde hair. She chuckled.

"What's funny?" Robert asked.

"Nothing," she answered with a smile.

His gaze was warm, with hints of the intimacy they had once shared. She couldn't help wondering what might have been if their lives had not drifted apart. *Could we get back together again? I might like that.*

"How did your day go?" he asked after they had ordered antipasti and wine.

"I went to the Uffizi. Had time for a long nap afterward. Thanks for leaving the ticket at will call, by the way. But before I got there, I ran into people running away from something going on near the Duomo. Someone told me there was an attack of some sort. Is that true? What's the story?"

"Actually, a murder. But there isn't much detail on the news. Just two guys who had come from early mass. Somebody stabbed them from behind. Nobody saw it happen, and the attackers had escaped, so the police don't seem to have any suspects."

"Is that possible? I mean, there must have been somebody who was a witness. Surely they saw something."

"Yeah, it doesn't make sense, does it? But that's all it said on the news. One dead, the other injured."

"But that's pretty brazen. To do it close to a church, I mean, and especially a church as historic and public as the Duomo. It just sounds so much like that story of the way Giuliano de Medici was murdered by the Pazzi conspirators."

Robert waved his hand, dismissing the thought. "Don't you think that's a little baroque?"

"No, seriously," Julia answered, leaning forward, elbows on the table, her hand toying with the stem of her wine glass. "In fact, one of the women I met in the *pasticceria* on the corner said the same thing. I mean, she thought of the Pazzi murder, too."

"More likely organized crime," Robert said. "Florence has had problems with that before. Don't you remember the Mafia attacks on the Uffizi a few years back?"

The stories had been in the news both in the United States and Europe. Julia had followed developments with shock and concern. "Weren't there a lot of assaults on historic and artistic sites in Italy back then?" she asked. "All involving car bombs?"

"Right. At the Uffizi, the bombs shattered glass throughout the museum. A few pieces in the collection were damaged or destroyed. Several people died."

"Do people still think there's a security problem?"

"Not so much from the local Mafia," Robert replied. "They eventually cut back on violence because of a political campaign against them. Now, it's criminal syndicates from other countries and drug and human trafficking rings throughout Italy. Sex trafficking is especially common—and ruthless. The syndicates don't care who is hurt. And the police don't seem to know how to control them."

"You sound like you take it personally."

"I do," he said, his voice tinged with anger. "That kind of crime is a disgrace to this beautiful city."

The emotion in his response didn't surprise Julia. It was so typical of Robert. In college, he had always been an activist, passionate about supporting social causes and issues he believed in. Righting wrongs wherever he thought they existed in society. *I guess he must have some things he's involved in here, too.*

The conversation had taken on a dark tone that threatened to spoil the evening. Both of them watched in silence as their waiter arrived with their entrees. Julia picked up her fork and smiled at Robert. "That's too much reality for me if you don't mind," she said. "Let's talk about something else."

"OK. Tell me more about what you're doing here. I thought you were pretty well established at that ad agency in Seattle,"

"I was. Used my background in art to do graphic design work. But I got bored. Restless, I guess. So I quit my job. I'm a freelance photographer and writer now. Rented out my house and stored all my belongings in my Mom's basement so I could spend the year traveling in Italy."

"Really? How did your mother feel about your being gone so long?"

"She was great. She even said if I decided to stay, she and my stepdad would come and visit me. She was kidding, but I think she's glad I have some happy memories of living here."

Julia stopped as the waiter cleared away the plates from their first course and then looked across the table at Robert. "That's enough about me. What are you working on now? Are you still freelancing? Or are you concentrating on fiction? A novel, maybe?"

His face brightened. "Short stories. I wrote one novel, but I seem to be more of a short story writer, I guess. Everything is set in Italy, of course. In the fifteenth century. For all its political intrigue, it was still a more hopeful era. Not happier, I suppose. Just less complicated."

"The time of the Medici family and their rivals?"

"Lorenzo mainly. At least as far as my stories are

concerned. And there were some wonderful alliances or battles among families whose names are still part of the Florentine scene. The Strozzi family, for example, built their great palace around that time. Did you know that Filippo Strozzi's heirs went bankrupt trying to realize his vision of having the largest palazzo in Florence? Deliberately larger than the Medici palace. He bought and demolished all kinds of buildings to make room for it."

"His heirs finished it? You mean he didn't live to see it?"

"No, he died a couple of years after the first foundation stone was laid. It wasn't completed for another 40 years or so."

"I didn't know that. What about the Pazzi? And the Pazzi Palace?"

"Back to the Pazzi, eh? You can't seem to get them out of your head today,"

"You have to admit the Pazzi conspiracy was one of the most memorable challenges to the Medici regime."

"Yes. Especially if people still bring it up in connection with recent crimes."

"But isn't that part of the charm of Florence? That it lives simultaneously in so many different historical realities?"

"True. I love that aspect of life here. And it's not just the reminders of the past that people find in events of the present. It's the actual look of the historic core. You can be walking down a very modern street--Via de' Tornabuoni, say, with all of its upscale businesses--and you turn onto a side alley that looks like it did centuries ago, with laundry hanging out of the windows and merchants tending to their small shops. It's a time warp. You feel like you are a part of that history."

Dinner was as delicious as Robert had promised. They chose the house specialties—insalata mista, spaghetti carbonara, and veal chops. The "Supertuscan" Chianti Robert selected to go with their meal left Julia a little light-headed. Robert insisted that they cap off the meal with tiramisu.

Stores in the historic center were closed when they left the restaurant, and there was a chill in the air, early enough in the year to be coat weather. They decided to go window shopping, starting with the Giorgio Armani and Enrico Coveri stores on Via della Vigna Nuova. At Julia's urging, they went from there to Via de' Tornabuoni, long the most fashionable commercial area in Florence, known for exquisite gloves, purses, shoes, and jewelry whose simple elegance was in stark contrast to some of the trendier clothing styles in streets nearby. They lingered laughing at mannequins posed arched-back and imperious in the windows of some of the high-end shops they passed.

In the streets near Via de' Tornabuoni, Florence's Renaissance past took up where twentieth-century commerce left off. "Here's a neighborhood that I find fascinating," Robert said, taking Julia's hand as they entered a narrow, twisting walkway with overhead passageways extending from one side wall to the other. They strolled along the same path that Dante, Michelangelo, Leonardo, and their contemporaries could have taken centuries before, its look not much altered. The sounds of domestic life could be heard from apartments along their way. The faint aromas of luscious dinners prepared earlier that night filled the air.

"Have you ever thought about coming back to

Florence?" Robert asked. "Not just to study or visit, I mean, but to live here?"

Julia didn't answer for a moment. She *had* thought about it, but for a long time, she had rejected the idea.

"Too many ghosts," she said.

"Ghosts?"

"Remembrances of things past. You can't go home again. You know. All the clichés. I would love to live here again, but I don't know if I could without remembering everything about how I once lived here before. What Bill and I did when we were together."

They continued walking along the narrow street, neither speaking. Finally, Robert asked, "What happened between you and Bill?"

"It's a long story," she answered. "I just didn't want to hurry into marriage. I was afraid I might repeat the mistake Mom made. You remember my telling you how she married when she was rather young and then went through a bitter divorce a few years after I was born? I just wanted to live life on my own for a while. Bill couldn't accept that, I guess." Her voice wavered as she added, "He ended our relationship by sending me the announcement of his engagement to someone else."

Robert was silent, hesitating before he spoke again. "That was pretty brutal. Is it still painful for you?"

"Yes." Her answer was so immediate and emphatic that she surprised herself. Before her trip, she thought she had moved beyond the details of her earlier life enough to confront her past without too much discomfort. But one day in Florence had resurrected the memories and the sadness that followed. That was the problem. She was afraid that staying longer might give all that even greater intensity.

"That's too bad," Robert said. "I mean, I love it here. I can't imagine ever leaving. Sometimes, I feel guilty about not wanting to go back to California and not having that connection with the place where I grew up. But when Dad died two years ago, there was just nothing left there for me. It probably sounds strange, but even though we hadn't seen each other much since Mother died—well, with him gone, I felt like I was an orphan. A grown-up orphan, maybe, but an orphan all the same. Without a base."

"Don't you feel a little homesick though?" Julia asked. "Even if you've lived here eight years or so, and it feels like home, it isn't really. I know it's your adopted country, but it's not the one that shaped who you are."

"If that's how I should feel about the place where I was born and grew up, shouldn't you feel that way about Florence?"

"Robert, I don't remember much about that time in my life. I was born in Florence but I lived here for only a few years while my father was conducting his business. I was a young child when my parents' marriage ended, and my mother took me back home to the States. Their breakup was pretty traumatic for me."

"Even so, this city has a special place in your past. Shouldn't it still be special to you?"

He was pressing the point, making Julia think about returning to Florence for a longer stay. "Are you trying to tell me something?" she laughed, teasing him into a response.

"Well," he said, "I admit I'm lonely sometimes. I've really been looking forward to your visit. It feels good to have you here. It would be great if you could stay here a little longer."

"Actually, the possibility has been on my mind lately," she answered. "But now that I'm here, everything seems so unsettling. I might be going through some sort of time lag. I just feel funny, somehow—strange—and it has to do with being back here and going to familiar places. I'll get over it."

She squeezed his hand, and he glanced over at her and smiled.

"Enough said for now, then."

They left the narrow passageway and found their way back to the Piazza della Signoria. Café Rivoire was still open, but the customers who could usually be seen drinking coffee and cocktails at the outdoor tables were no longer there. The evening was left to a few strolling tourists like themselves and three boys who looked about eight to ten years old who were playing a shorthanded game of *calcio*, racing from one side of the piazza to the other. The feeling that Florence could be home again, not just a travel destination, was palpable.

She caught herself composing the moment as a photograph—the boys frozen in their leaps and high kicks, the tourists in the piazza glancing back at them, smiling, the moonlight glancing off the replica of the statue of David that guarded the Palazzo Vecchio, and the lights of the shops around the piazza a sparkling necklace tying the scene together.

"I do see why you love it here," she said. And, this time, Robert squeezed her hand.

CHAPTER 5

After dinner, back in her hotel, Julia was tired but too keyed up from the day's events to go to bed immediately. She was still having trouble adjusting to European time. Settling onto the overstuffed chair in the corner of her room, she sized up her accommodations. She hadn't paid them much attention in the morning, and in the evening, she had been in a hurry to get dressed for dinner with Robert.

Her quarters were stylishly furnished and functional, with a king bed at one end and a large wooden wardrobe and a desk at the other. The chair where she was sitting, along with a matching ottoman and a floor lamp, provided a comfortable area for relaxing. Pastel colors on the bed pillows and spread were picked up in floral designs on the furniture and the window coverings. White walls brightened the decor and made the space seem larger.

It was just right for her. In the days ahead, she would clear the desk for her camera and supplies and string her travel clothesline in the bathroom so she could hang her laundry to dry after she had washed it in the sink. Until then, she'd just relax and enjoy the cozy feeling of her room.

What she loved most were the two windows, large and dominating, that rose from about waist height to a couple of feet below the high ceilings. Very Italian. Their glass frames enclosed louvered privacy panels, fastened in the daytime to keep out light when the external Persian shutters were open. Only in the heat of summer would the external shutters be shut during the day as well to insulate the room from the temperatures outside and hold in the cool air as long as possible.

She got up briefly to retrieve her notebooks from her luggage, putting them on the desk alongside her camera bag. Satisfied that she had everything ready for the work that lay ahead, she thought about what she would need to do on the assignment that had brought her to Florence, a photo essay on the city at the turn of the millennium.

While other writers were likely to focus on the Great Jubilee's impact on Rome, she had pitched a different angle to a travel magazine whose editor had been intrigued by her background and her plan to describe her impressions upon returning to the country of her birth. The congruence of her pilgrimage with the church's summons of religious tourists promised an unusual appeal. Her arrival in mid-March was a perfect time to be in Italy—before high season when most tourists typically came, early enough to have an article in print for travelers arriving in 2000. The weather was likely to be blustery, rainy, and cool, but no worse than back home in Seattle.

She walked over to one of the windows and opened the outer shutters. Leaning forward, she propped her elbows on the sill and looked down on the area fronting the hotel. Despite the chill in the air, it was a calm and beautiful evening. Dinner with Robert had settled and relaxed her. Maybe her complicated memories of Florence weren't so troubling after all.

In the empty piazza below, a man scurried into view. Dressed in a black jacket, T-shirt, and trousers, he blended into the shadows, but his face was visible: dark hair, dark eyes. Julia sensed that she was the only one watching his movements. All the other windows in the buildings surrounding the square were closed. At this time of night, probably everyone else was sleeping.

The man looked back toward the street bordering the piazza as though someone was following him. Then he looked toward the other side of the open space.

He can't be trying to find other ways out of here. She smiled at his almost-theatrical confusion, looking first in one direction and then in the other, back and forth. There were only two possibilities for entry and exit. Clearly, he didn't want to take either. He turned frantically toward the hotel, looked up, and saw Julia staring at him. He scowled and pointed at her.

She felt her heartbeat quicken and leaned away from the window so she couldn't be seen. What if he found his way into the hotel? Would he know where she was and how to get to her room? Its location at the end of a long, relatively dark corridor had been appealing to her when she first arrived because of its promise of quiet and privacy. Now she realized there was no one around to hear her if she needed help. She suddenly felt vulnerable and alone.

Listening for noises in the hallway outside, she heard a few footsteps and a door opening nearby. Finally, there was nothing except the sound of her rapid breathing.

She returned to see if the man was still in the piazza.

He was gone. She closed the outer shutters, and locked the glass window and privacy panel. Remembering a precaution her mother had taught her, she got up and carried the desk chair over to the door to her room, slipping the back of it under the inside doorknob. It was a simple but effective way of barring entry.

That should keep any intruders out, she thought, feeling a little more secure. After she undressed, she turned out the light and got into bed. "What a day!" she sighed.

Responding to a need she hadn't felt since childhood, she closed her eyes and prayed that the next day would be less stressful and frightening. But she couldn't erase the image of the man from her thoughts. There was no doubt about it: he hadn't wanted anyone to see him, and he knew that she was a witness to his actions. Did he glimpse enough of her to recognize her if they encountered each other another time? She knew she wouldn't forget him, or the look on his face. Her photographer's eye again.

Tossing and turning well into the night, she finally fell into a troubled sleep.

CHAPTER 6

Piero Manca looked in the mirror and adjusted his tie, admiring the suit he donned every morning when he came to work as a bellman at the hotel. After six months on the job, he still loved the sense of importance he felt when he stepped into the lobby in his handsome uniform and assumed his place near the front door.

"*Eh*, Piero." The hotel manager motioned him over to the reception desk at the far end of the lobby. "I need you to bring in some chairs from the roof garden. Some of our guests apparently left them out there last night. Not sure why. I guess they stayed out there after dark, having cocktails. We can't let the chairs get exposed to the sun, and our maintenance staff is busy with other repairs."

Piero didn't mind. He loved the terrace in the roof garden. With its breathtaking view of the Duomo seemingly floating over the rooftops of Florence, it was his favorite place in the hotel. He sometimes stopped to linger there on his own, on his way back from delivering luggage or messages to rooms in that wing of the building. It gave him a few moments of relaxation and a chance to marvel once again at that remarkable vista.

As he rounded the turn from the stairs leading up to the roof, he saw the door to the garden was ajar.

"*Allo?*" he said, peeking around the door as he looked outside. He could never tell when hotel guests might be up there, or what they might be doing, even in the morning. It was a place that invited trysts, and more than once, he had come upon couples ardently embracing there.

This time, there was no one.

"*Accidenti,*" he said as he caught his breath. Several chairs were stacked against the side wall, and it appeared that they had served as a way to raise someone high enough to see the roofs of surrounding buildings—a precarious perch. Piero instinctively looked down to the alley below, fearing he might see evidence of a misstep or an accident. The only damage he could see was that some of the tiles on top of the wall were slightly askew.

He sighed with relief. *No one has fallen, thank God.* But why had they engaged in such a foolish act? It wasn't necessary. One could easily get a better view by climbing the stairs in the Duomo's campanile.

He tucked a couple of chairs under his arms and carried them back into the room adjoining the terrace. It took several trips, but finally, he returned all the furniture to their usual seating arrangement inside, leaving only a pair of patio chairs outside. Closing the door to the roof garden, he followed the hallway to the elevator and returned to the lobby.

CHAPTER 7

Julia slept late again. When she awoke in the middle of the morning and saw the security system she had improvised for her room the night before, she winced. *Boy, that was an overreaction.* In the daytime, it was easier to set aside the fear she had felt looking out the window at the strange man in the piazza. She dressed and headed to the hotel dining room. Over brunch, she organized her thoughts into an itinerary of places she wanted to visit and what she needed to photograph at each step along the way.

The day that lay ahead would be busy, the first of several in which she would size up the photo possibilities in the heart of Florence. During her stay, she would compile a collection of images, photographing as many sites as she could, recording her thoughts and impressions in a notebook.

With her tripod and camera bag loaded with her trusty Giorgetto Giugiaro-designed Nikon F5, plus film and lenses, she headed out of the hotel. Within minutes she had arrived at the Piazza del Duomo and the Baptistry opposite the Cathedral's front door. She could see no evidence of the attack that had been the topic of so much conversation the day before. The police had obviously finished their investigation, and the scene had been restored to its quotidian functions.

She stopped to admire the exterior of the Duomo for a few moments, unsure of how it would fit into the theme of her photo essay. This morning, she decided, her time might be better spent becoming reacquainted with Florence's most famous church.

Its spacious interior was filled with more tourists than usual, their visits no doubt postponed by the police closure the day before. Julia stood close to the high altar beneath the massive dome and gazed upward. "Awesome," she whispered as she marveled at the feat of architecture and engineering that Brunelleschi had managed to pull off, closing the space that had stood open for years. Her rapt admiration of it was interrupted by a tour guide lecturing to a group of American tourists clustering around her at the front of the sanctuary.

After yesterday, I've had enough of tourist groups for a while.

She looked around for a place where she could continue to enjoy the church in relative solitude. Glancing over at one of the side chapels in the apse, she began to move toward it and then stopped, startled by the face she saw watching her from the chapel. It was the man she had seen the night before in the piazza outside her hotel. Had he recognized her as well? He started to walk toward her.

Backing away, she turned and hurried toward the tour group, hiding behind a large pillar and moving quickly behind the Americans until she found a side exit onto the street. Once out the door, she ran to her hotel, dashing through its entrance without looking back. When she reached her room, she locked the door and stood staring at it, momentarily safe, her heart pounding. The protective instinct that had propelled her out of the Duomo transformed itself from strength into paralysis. She felt even more defenseless than she had the night before.

Lingering over *pranzo* in the hotel restaurant, Julia had time to think. Why did she succumb so easily to anxiety when she was under pressure or in tense situations? "When are you going to grow up and stop being so afraid of everything?" Bill had said angrily in one of the arguments they had as their relationship deteriorated.

She had fought back, denying his criticism, but deep inside, she knew he was right. She had been panicky and nervous since childhood after her parents had separated, and neither of them had noticed her distress or tried to comfort her. They had been too caught up in their own emotional turmoil. Bill hadn't helped. When they first met, he relished his role as her older, wiser protector. She became dependent on his strength, sustaining her.

She sighed and rubbed her forehead. *What's the worst that can happen if I run into that man again? If I'm out in the open, he won't do anything. Maybe I'll even find out what he really wants.*

Just because he had scowled at her and tried to approach her in the Duomo didn't mean that he actually remembered her or meant her any harm, she decided. And sitting in her hotel room wasn't going to complete the professional assignment that had brought her to Florence.

Sipping an espresso at the end of her meal, she concentrated on writing the first entry in her travel journal. It comforted her to get her thoughts—and fears—on paper. Her regular habit of keeping a record of her observations and feelings always had a calming effect on her. She needed that now.

Journal

Saw Robert. Looks great, as always. Handsome and funny. Gave me a great idea for the millennium article. Towers in the neighborhoods.

Spent this morning coming up with ideas for a photo shoot. Lots of winding, picturesque side streets. I never tire of Florence —still one of the most beautiful cities in the world, no matter how many tourists clog the streets and shops. They're already here, and it's only March.

Will look into the other historical angles Robert suggested when I have more energy.

Last night we went to dinner at Paoli, a few blocks from the hotel. Lots of atmosphere, great entrees and a fabulous dessert cart. The waiter loved to show off his command of languages. Spoke fluent English with us, and then turned to the next table and spoke Japanese to the Japanese tourists there. All of the women in the restaurant got flowers. Something about International Women's Day.

I love being with Robert again. I wonder if we could recapture what we felt for each other in college.

Came back late. Roamed around the hotel a little before I returned to my room. Checked out the roof garden down the hall. Has an absolutely incredible view of the Duomo. Almost felt I could reach out and touch it.

She paused a moment before adding the last line:

Something about this place gives me the creeps.

Feeling more relaxed, she tucked the leather-bound notebook into a side compartment in her camera bag. The rest of the day would be devoted to studying other neighborhoods in the historic center to see if there were any renovations still underway there and to find locations that would bring back her own memories. Her personal connection to Florence had helped get her the commission for the article she was writing. She had to be open to the complicated feelings that would bring that connection to life for her, and for her readers.

Her first photo shoot would be at Santa Maria Novella, the Dominican basilica across a piazza from the train station. In the research she had done before her return to Italy, it was the restoration project in Florence that was mentioned most often.

Her way there took her along a narrow thoroughfare with sidewalks scarcely large enough to accommodate the flow of pedestrian traffic, past several small shops and a couple of large department stores before she arrived at the basilica. The area fronting it was beautiful but somewhat cramped, confined by the neighborhood surrounding it.

Pacing back and forth, she studied the façade, searching for a fresh shot of the church and its complex of courtyards and cloisters. She found a location that provided the perspective she wanted. She had to be careful not to bother any workmen who might still be busy with outside renovations. And it wasn't likely that she would be allowed inside the church if it was under repair. Even asking might require negotiations with municipal authorities.

Taking her camera out of her equipment bag and attaching the lens she wanted, then extending the tripod, she went to work. Next was the part of photography she liked most. Composition, for her, was the true creative act. Alternately standing and kneeling, she captured the scene with a rapid-fire succession of shots. When she was done, she began packing up her gear. As she readied to leave, she saw a priest coming toward her across the piazza.

"*Ciao*," he said, greeting her with a broad smile.

"*Ciao*," Julia answered, adding an apology in her rusty Italian in case she had intruded in some way on the project or the work of the parish.

"There is no problem," the priest assured her, responding in English. "I saw you out here, and I could tell you are a professional photographer, not a tourist. I was curious why you want pictures before the restoration is done."

"I'm doing a photo essay about the preparations being made for the pilgrimage and the beginning of the new millennium," she explained.

"Ah, *si*," he said, nodding appreciatively. "It is not so easy to capture her, is it?" he said, pointing back at the church.

"No. It's hard to find a spot that hasn't been used a thousand times before. There just aren't that many options. Why was the church built in this neighborhood?"

"It was the reverse of that. The neighborhood grew around the church complex as the city's housing and commercial needs expanded outward."

"I love it," Julia said, glancing back at the façade, its green and white marble glistening. "Somehow, it gives me more of a sense of the scale of the city in the past. If it's possible to see what is being done, I will come back. But I want to do some exterior shots of other buildings first."

"I will be glad to help you," the priest said eagerly.

"And if you have trouble getting permission, let me know. I'm sure we can make arrangements." He winked. Arrangements. The Italian way of getting around the bureaucratic web of paperwork that often seemed to ensnarl public and private transactions. Julia thanked the priest, promising to return soon.

He hesitated and, extending his arm toward her, signaled for her to pause a bit longer before she left.

"*Signorina*, I'm just a priest, not a professional photographer, but may I make a suggestion?"

"Of course." She threw her camera bag over her shoulder and waited. He bowed his head before he spoke again.

"The preparations for the Jubilee are almost finished, as you know. There's not much left to photograph of the work that is still to be done." He smiled, obviously eager to propose another idea for her consideration. "The pilgrimage is meant to bring change to the lives of those who participate in it. Change to people, not just to buildings. Is there a way to show that?"

Julia nodded. There might be something in the approach he was suggesting, but it wasn't what she had pitched to the magazine editor. And pilgrims had probably not yet begun to arrive, so shots of tourists already in Italy wouldn't necessarily demonstrate the kind of transformation he had in mind. Still, she didn't want to seem like she was dismissing his idea entirely. "That would be an interesting sidelight for my photo shoot. Thank you. I'll consider it."

She said goodbye to the priest and walked back through the streets she had followed earlier. Her plan for the rest of the afternoon was to visit the part of Florence that had more meaning for her personally. Wandering past the Palazzo Vecchio, she found her way across the river to the neighborhood in the Oltrarno, where Bill had maintained an apartment, and the two of them had spent much of their time together. Later, she would try to find locations in the part of the city where her mother had told her their family lived when she was a child.

She took a few photos of buildings along her way, but she could tell they lacked any human interest. The afternoon siesta, well underway when she had left her hotel after *pranzo*, was now coming to an end. Activity was starting up again along the streets, so she stopped at a *pasticceria* and ordered an espresso and a pastry. Taking her place at an outside table, she watched tourists on their way to the Palazzo Pitti and some of the craft shops close by. She drank her coffee and thought about what the priest at Santa Maria Novella had said.

Photographing buildings would be easy but too removed from the deeper meaning of a pilgrimage or the dawn of a new millennium. The pilgrimage angle was looming larger in her mind now. The priest was right. What she needed were more images of people. She had seen visitors already in Florence. Even with the Great Jubilee celebrations several months away, many of them could be there as pilgrims. The narrative accompanying her photos could describe how those coming to Italy in the upcoming festival year were affected in different ways by encounters with sites along the pilgrimage route. Even before the Jubilee began, churches and monuments could foster reflection and maybe even change in individuals who came to see them. Focusing on personal transformation could also frame the story she would tell about her own journey.

Pulling the notebook out of her camera bag, she

quickly jotted down a few observations, and then, more slowly, she put together a detailed outline of likely scenes and themes. When she had finished, she felt energized by the possibilities of the project. Even better, she realized the preoccupations with events that had seemed to threaten her safety earlier in the day had completely faded away.

This is going to be great! She leaned back in her chair and thought of the days ahead.

It was a good way to spend the afternoon.

CHAPTER 8

Piero, at first, didn't make the connection between disrupted tiles on the balcony wall of the roof garden and the chairs that had been stacked on the terrace the night before. It came to him later as he listened to the hotel bartender tell the manager about the pieces of broken terra cotta he had found in the alley on that side of the hotel on his way to work that afternoon.

"How could those have come loose?" the bartender had wondered. "They were installed new just last month," he said, recalling that they were part of the renovations that had been underway in the building next door. The new owner wasn't known to many yet. He was a phantom, the subject of much speculation among all the merchants in the neighborhood, even more so after he had invested in a restoration of an old warehouse that had stood neglected for years.

The bartender continued his description of his strange find. "The roof tile couldn't have been weakened by the weather yet. It had to have been struck or kicked by someone or something," he asserted.

Or by someone jumping onto it, Piero thought. He vowed to check out the possibility as soon as he could find time.

He had trouble containing his excitement as he went through the day's duties. With an increasing number of guests arriving to stay in the hotel, the manager kept him busy carrying luggage, running errands, and delivering messages.

Near the end of his shift, he finally found the time to slip up to the roof garden once again. The patio chairs were in place as he had left them in the morning, but they weren't the focus of his interest anymore. He strode directly to the side wall. Its surface was cracked at exactly the spot where the chairs had been stacked the night before. Directly opposite, the top of the wall surrounding the balcony on the adjacent building had several missing tiles.

Could someone have leaped from one roof to the other? But why would they do that? A person would have been mad to try, or at least reckless. And how would anyone have gotten out of the building next door once they were over on the other side?

It was too much for Piero. He scratched his head and pondered the image in his head of someone leaping from one wall to the next for no good reason.

He decided he wouldn't tell the hotel manager what he had discovered and what he suspected. It would sound a little crazy, he knew, and in any case, he enjoyed knowing something that no one else knew for now. *Besides, it might be worth something to someone if I kept it to myself.*

That he could be in danger if he didn't tell someone didn't cross his mind.

CHAPTER 9

When Julia returned to her hotel late in the afternoon, there was a note from Robert at the desk.

"Call me immediately."

Sounds important. I wonder what's up?

She called him from the phone down the corridor from her room.

"Pronto," Robert answered in Italian after only a couple of rings. He sounded relieved to hear Julia's voice.

"Where have you been?" he asked.

"Exploring the city. Why do you ask?"

"You need to get out of that hotel. As quickly as possible."

"Why?" Julia began to feel her panic return as she sensed the concern in Robert's voice.

"You don't have a phone in your room, do you? I assume you're calling from a hall phone?"

"Yes, that's right. What are you getting at?"

"I can't explain now. Just get your stuff together, and

I'll find you another place for a few nights. I'll meet you in the lobby in an hour."

"Can it be nearby? This is the neighborhood where I want to be. It's close to all the sites I want to photograph."

"I'll see what I can do. Just get ready to move. I'll see you soon."

The click of the phone as Robert hung up left her sitting in silence. Replacing the receiver, she opened the door slowly and looked down the corridor toward the entrance to the roof garden. Evening approached. It was growing dark inside the hotel as well as outside.

She hurried back to her room and began packing.

Julia could see Robert pacing back and forth as the elevator arrived at the lobby and its glass doors slid open. She was carrying a single overnight bag.

"I'm ready," she said. "But I'm not leaving for good. You're going to have to explain to me why this is necessary."

Robert stared at her, exasperated, and ran his hand through his hair. "All right," he mumbled. "But not here. Leave your room key at the desk and pick up your passport. Tell them you'll be staying with a friend tonight. I'll get the car ready."

Minutes later, they were in Robert's Fiat, inching down the narrow side streets on their way to the roads that would take them to the more modern areas beyond the city walls.

"Where are we going?" she asked. "I thought I would be moving to another hotel in the city center."

"You will," he answered. "We're going to my apartment first, and then I'll take you back to another hotel—a *pensione* on the Lungarno. It's close to everything, and it's the kind of place you'll like."

"So why didn't we just go immediately there? It couldn't have been more than a few streets away."

"I need to talk to you first. Someplace where I know we won't be overheard. And I didn't want to risk the possibility that we might be followed from your old place to the new one."

"What's going on? Is all this really necessary?"

"Maybe it is, and maybe it isn't. I'm not sure myself. I just don't want to take any chances." He took his eyes off the road long enough to glance over at Julia. "I just didn't want to risk your safety."

"Risk? How?"

"You are staying in a part of Florence that may be in the middle of some sort of criminal activity. And your room is in a section of the hotel that could be an access point."

"Access to what? And what kind of criminal activity? Is the hotel engaging in it?"

"No. The hotel and the buildings around it are just a convenient location. I can't say right now what's happening nearby or if something more is going to happen. All I know is, whatever is going on may be linked to organized crime. And the activity I'm concerned about may have to do with a building near the hotel where you've been staying. But I can't tell you much more than that."

"How do you know all this? And why did you have me move out all of a sudden? Was something about to happen?"

"I have a friend who works for the police. He's a source

for me." He looked at her and then back at the busy road ahead of him.

"Okay, you need to know something about me that I haven't told you before," he said. "I don't just write short stories about Florence in the Renaissance. I also do investigations of unsolved crimes. I mean, I've written some articles about modern Italian crime—under a pseudonym. The guy who told me about all this—the one who is with the police—is someone I've been getting information from for a long time. The building I mentioned is under surveillance. But with the killing in the Duomo yesterday…"

"Is that connected to all this?" Julia couldn't help but interrupt.

"Maybe."

"So why did you dismiss what I said about it last night." she asked angrily.

"I didn't dismiss what you said. I just thought the allusion you made to the Pazzi conspiracy was farfetched. But the attack at the Duomo was probably related to things going on in the city, and it was definitely meant to send a message."

"Why did I have to get out of my room so quickly? I don't see the connection with me."

"You don't personally have any connection. You're just staying in a part of the hotel close to the other buildings, and as long as you are there, I'm worried that you might become involved."

"Meaning what?"

His voice rising, Robert tried to explain. "Look, what I'm trying to say is that I've heard that something is about to happen in the neighborhood, near the section of the hotel where you're staying. If you get in the way of whatever it is—you could be hurt."

"This is too incredible. I can't believe it."

"Think for a minute. Can you honestly say you haven't noticed something about staying in that room that made you feel you were being watched?"

Julia caught her breath. "Well, something did happen that I've been meaning to mention to you, but it just seemed too crazy." And for the rest of their drive, she told him about the man she had seen in the piazza outside her room and in the Duomo.

CHAPTER 10

Robert's apartment in a neighborhood just off the autostrada had little of the warmth or personality she would have expected of the place he called home. The room he had rented off the university campus when they were students had been full of comfortable furniture and stacked with books and memorabilia. He hadn't brought any of that with him to Florence, which wasn't particularly surprising, given the expense that would have been involved in moving all of it to Italy. But his current living space was almost literally the exact opposite of what he would have preferred earlier in his life. It was a spartan, two-bedroom flat decorated in an efficient "hotel modern" look that suggested the furniture went with the apartment. Maybe, she thought, it also had to do with the need for anonymity surrounding his crime investigations.

As Robert went into the small kitchen to pour glasses of wine for the two of them, Julia peeked into the bedrooms. One was clearly where Robert slept. The other was his office. Beneath the only window in that room was a plain, utilitarian desk, just large enough to hold both a computer and a printer. Two bookcases to the side of the desk held an array of novels, reference books, and historical volumes Robert obviously kept close by to consult while he was writing. Reams of paper and cartons of printer supplies were stacked carefully on the bottom shelves. On the opposite wall was a bright red couch and framed photos of the Tuscan countryside, splashes of color in an otherwise dreary room.

She turned around to find Robert behind her, a glass of wine in each hand.

"Now you see why I don't spend much time here. Actually, it's good for writing. The sofa bed came with the apartment, but I kind of like it. And the view out the window in the living room is nice. Not too distracting. Housing is expensive in Florence, so I feel lucky to have this. But it's not home, I know that."

She took the wine he offered and clicked his glass with hers. A friendly toast. "*Cin cin*. Now, let's talk."

Under other circumstances, she would have loved the evening. Robert prepared their meal. Nothing special, just what he had intended to have for himself: Tuscan salad, pasta cooked in olive oil and butter. Bread and cheese, fruit for dessert, and Chianti.

Over dinner, they talked. While Julia conceded she was frightened to think what might have happened if she had stayed in the hotel in a room where she admittedly had already experienced a sense of foreboding, she still had trouble accepting all that Robert was suggesting. Even worse, there were things about his life in Florence that he had concealed from her.

Had he spent the years since he graduated from college teaching part-time, writing short stories, and working on a novel about the Medici? Yes, teaching was an important source of income, but his short stories and the novel weren't the only focus of his work.

Had he led art history tours around Florence to support himself while he waited for his first big break as a writer? Yes, especially early in his stay—before police investigations became a more reliable source of income.

Had his circle of friends been largely American expatriates and American university exchange professors, preoccupied mainly with art, literature, and music? True, in part. Some of his friends were American or British academics, but his world also revolved around people he had met in investigations of the dark side of Italian politics and crime.

And who were the "friends" he had come to rely on? It would be safer for him not to tell her, he said. What kinds of crimes had he investigated? He wouldn't say.

She just had to trust him, he said. At some point, he promised, he would tell her everything. But he couldn't right now. She just had to believe him when he said that he would make sure that she was never in harm's way.

"This is crazy," she said when he finished his description of his life and his concerns. "You're asking me to trust you when you haven't been entirely honest with me up until now. And this story about my being in danger from some vague threat from organized crime.... I don't know what to say about that. It's just too improbable."

Conversation for the rest of dinner was strained. Robert struggled to get back to the playful tone they'd enjoyed with each other the night before, but Julia didn't respond. After a while, they sat in silence. She sipped the wine he had poured and gazed absently at the sparse furnishings of the place Robert called home.

When it was clear that they had both said all that they had to say to each other, Robert drove her back to the historic part of Florence and carried her bag to the reception desk on the second floor of the *pensione* where he had made reservations for her. He lingered until she finished checking in at the desk, watching to make sure there were no problems with her late arrival.

"I'll call you tomorrow," he said as she turned to take the elevator up to her room.

"Okay."

"You'll be fine. I promise. We'll talk some more."

"Okay."

He leaned forward and kissed her on the cheek, gently squeezing her arm. She stepped into the elevator and watched him silently as the door closed.

Once in her room, her bag unpacked, she sat for a long time in the overstuffed chair that crowded the space at the side of the room. She fell asleep there, pondering all that had happened during the day.

CHAPTER 11

Robert hurried through the narrow passage between buildings just off the piazza. As he approached the carefully hidden entry to the basement of one of them, he slowed his pace and pulled the hood of his jacket over his face, wrapping the rest of the bulky fabric around him. The disguise that had once seemed unnecessarily theatrical now felt more comfortable and even necessary. As safe as he had always believed he was in the company of the others who were as committed as he was to exposing and fighting crime in the city, recent events reminded him that the safety of all of them depended on their secrecy. And he understood why. Anonymity protected them.

Using the rhythmic code that signaled membership in the group, he tapped on the door. It opened just a crack. Into the darkness, he muttered the password for the month. A shadowy figure nodded to him as he stepped inside.

"Are the others here?" he asked as the two passed through the low-ceilinged storage area. Filled with plastic containers, cardboard boxes and unused furniture, the space concealed the location of the other rooms deeper in the building.

"Yes. They came immediately when they got your message."

Robert bowed his head as he entered the meeting room, an act of greeting and obedience. They were all there, wearing the simple cowled overcoats that were the symbol of their community of purpose. Thirty of them, sitting in a tight circle, as was their custom. He settled into the empty chair on the side opposite the doorway, the place reserved for the one who called the group together.

How did he have the courage—some might say the audacity—to summon the others for a special meeting? While there was no hierarchy among them and no specific leaders, Robert typically deferred to the others. Usually, he sat quietly, observing and listening. It was their city, after all. He was just an adopted son.

Their group was modeled on secret organizations in the past, although its members rejected the rigid structure and the mystical trappings of their predecessors. There were no initiation rites, no rituals, and no mysterious robes or symbols. None of that seemed appropriate to men in the late twentieth century. They simply shared a strength of commitment, a unifying feeling that the wisdom and the integrity of the old days were being eroded by corruption and crime in the present. They vowed to fight the evil they saw around them. And to that end, they came together when anyone among them felt there was a need for action.

Robert was convinced it was now. *I have to speak up. Tell them what I have learned.* He pulled back his hood, cleared his throat, and spoke, nervously at first. "I'm sure you all know—or suspect—who was responsible for the attack in front of the Duomo?"

They nodded.

"And one of us is dead. I've heard that the other was severely wounded, too. But he will recover."

"Is he safe in the hospital?"

"He should be. The police are guarding his room day and night. Still, our enemies have ways of getting around that kind of protection."

"Surely you didn't gather us here just to tell us what we already knew?"

Robert has expected a challenge. *Of course, they would have questions.* He was ready.

"No. I called you together because I think this attack must lead to a new phase in our mission. We need to decide what we will do next. And do it quickly."

"That may be true," said the one whose voice always seemed to carry more weight among the others even though he was one of the younger men in the group. "But what convinces you that this might be a critical moment? What makes it so?"

"Because of the location and the manner of the attack," Robert answered, "I don't think their assault on two of our members in front of the Duomo was done without weighing the message it would send. Making us think of other periods of political upheaval in the past when there were challenges to the order of things. They obviously know who we are and what we are doing. So it was a warning—telling us what they are willing to do to make us stop."

The others were quiet, listening. A few nodded their heads. Most looked intently at Robert, waiting for him to continue. He cleared his throat again, ready to share his greatest fear. "I also have reason to believe that when they attack again, it will not only be at members of our group. They may also strike..." he added with a catch in his voice, thinking of Julia, "at those closest to us."

I'm going to have to be away from her for a while when I most want to be with her. But it's for her safety.

Silence filled the room for several moments until an older member of the society spoke, his voice weary but firm. "We have always known that there are dangers in what we are doing. So we do need to be ready. It's time to plan our next move." He pointed at Robert. "We are all concerned about crime in Florence, but your determination to learn more about the activities we are now trying to put an end to is invaluable to our mission. What have you discovered recently?"

This was the outcome Robert wanted. He looked around the room as the others leaned forward to hear him speak.

"We should pay more attention to the comings and goings in the buildings in the tower neighborhoods, he said. "Especially the empty ones. They're not so empty after all."

CHAPTER 12

It wasn't the first time that Piero had stayed in the hotel after his shift was over, but he usually let someone know where he was going. This time, after he left the jacket of his uniform in the staff closet behind the front desk, he waited until the hotel manager was occupied with checking in a new guest and slipped unnoticed down the hallway toward the stairway leading to the upper floors of the hotel.

Dusk had begun to settle on the city. Piero's first instinct as he walked into the open area on the roof was to check the cracked tiles on the rim of the garden wall. Small fragments of baked clay were lying on the terrace, and the terra cotta atop the wall enclosing the opposite roof was slightly broken. Still, as best he could tell, there had been no major additional damage since the last time he was there. Apparently, whatever had dislodged the tiles hadn't happened again.

He settled in a chair at the corner of the terrace. The top of the Duomo loomed in the distance, its size making it seem closer than it really was. Noise from cars and motorbikes coursing through nearby streets drifted up to his location, but it seemed a far-off distraction. Piero felt the serenity of the setting and contemplated what he should do next.

Sounds of a struggle in the alley below interrupted his thoughts. He rose and walked over to the side wall of the roof garden. Looking down, he saw several figures moving along the narrow passageway separating the hotel from the building next door. Two of them were smaller and appeared to be resisting being pulled by the others. A door opened and all struggled inside.

Something's wrong down there. I have to find out what's going on. Alarmed, he returned to the lobby, hurried through the hotel entrance, and ran over to the vacant warehouse. He looked cautiously into the empty passage and entered it slowly, quietly, listening for the sounds of anyone approaching. When he arrived at the door the others had entered a few minutes earlier, he looked back and forth to be sure he was alone and knelt next to the door, hoping to hear what was going on within. Several minutes passed.

Suddenly, he was pulled up from his kneeling position, but he couldn't see his attacker. Pain and fear combined as he struggled to escape the grasp of someone very large and very strong, lifting him and carrying him farther into the darkness. He tried to cry out, but he was gripped so tightly around the neck he couldn't speak. The pressure cut off his breath as well. Flailing weakly, he felt his strength ebb. And then all went dark.

CHAPTER 13

*D*anger.

It was the first word that came to mind when Julia awoke the next morning. She had likely been at personal risk until yesterday, and, no matter how she felt about the fact that Robert had concealed some details of his life from her, he had gone out of his way to remove her from what he thought was a potentially harmful situation. Their bond was still strong. When she saw him again, she would have to make sure he knew how grateful she was.

For today, her photo essay would take a back seat to other questions she now had. In place of fear, she was now driven by curiosity. It was time for a little investigating. Maybe she would find out more about what Robert suspected was going on in the area around the hotel where she had spent her first two nights in Florence.

Her thoughts kept wandering back to what Robert had told her about the illegal activity in parts of the city. Where could she find out more about crimes that had been committed in the last few years there—ones that might have been the subject of his investigations and reports?

Not the library, certainly. Information wouldn't be current enough there. Newspaper archives? That would take too much time, much of it probably leading to wasted effort. The local police? That might attract too much attention. And maybe she'd run into Robert's mysterious informant before she was ready to talk to him. The U.S. Consulate? Julia wasn't sure they'd be able to tell her what she needed to know about local criminal activities.

And then it came to her. The best choice to start, she decided, was with Carlo, a professor who had been part of the circle she and Bill had cultivated when they were students. Even though he had been more Bill's friend than hers, she knew she could be candid with him about both her reason for being in Florence and the concerns she had about her safety. Since his courses covered the social and political history of modern Italy, he might know about police investigations in the city. She wouldn't tell him about Robert or his concerns, she decided. She could just allude to "rumors" about the neighborhood that she had heard from other guests in the hotel after they had all learned about the murder near the Duomo. An event that dramatic would logically have raised questions in the minds of anyone staying nearby.

I'll call him this morning. If I don't get answers right away, I'll be distracted all day anyway, and won't be able to get on with my project.

Carlo seemed pleased to get her phone call. He hadn't heard from Bill in several years, he said. Julia explained that she and Bill were no longer together, which caused an awkward pause in their conversation, but once she made it clear she had a business reason to see him, the awkwardness went away. Not that he would have assumed she had a romantic reason for calling. Carlo was one of several gay men who were part of the circle of friends she and Bill had known at the university.

"Let's have lunch!" he suggested. "Just like the old days. I know a place over near the Pitti Palace, a short distance from the Ponte Vecchio. That's close to the *pensione* where you're staying. It won't be hard for you to get there."

Julia was relieved that the call went so well. She was eager to see Carlo and maybe begin to make sense of all that she had learned from Robert. She could spend the rest of the morning scoping out other places to photograph. But first, she wanted to make another entry in her journal.

Journal

I don't know where to start. I'm in a room at another hotel. Apparently a place where Robert stayed when he first came to Florence. Nothing fancy. Just a pensione. Checked in late. I spent the evening at Robert's apartment. Wish I could say I feel good about it. I'm glad he cares enough about me to want me out of the danger he thinks I'm in, but there's just something strange about the story he tells me. Or maybe it's just hard for me to accept that he isn't exactly the man I thought he was and has a life that is in some ways so unexpectedly different. He moves in circles where he knows a lot about the Italian underworld for reasons that somehow just don't ring true to me. And who is this mysterious friend who is his connection with all of this? It's like finding out he's somebody else and the person I used to know no longer exists.

Carlo was already at the restaurant, sitting at an outside table, watching the crowds of tourists passing by. He rose to greet her as she approached his table.

"Ciao!" he said, smiling as he grabbed her hand and kissed it, and then he leaned forward and kissed her on both cheeks. With a flourish, he pulled out a chair and invited her to sit. Julia couldn't help but smile. Carlo was older than she was by at least twenty years and had an infectious enthusiasm about everything that had always amused Bill and delighted her. His was not the demeanor of the average university professor.

The warmth of his welcome put Julia immediately at ease. It was like old times. Except for Bill's absence. Mercifully, Carlo didn't bring that up.

Motioning to the waiter for menus, he glanced at Julia. "So, what brings you to Florence again?" he asked.

She described her photo essay and its theme, and he nodded approvingly.

"That will be interesting to read. Promise me you'll send me a copy when it appears."

Julia laughed. "Of course. I may even send you a copy before it appears, so you can catch any mistakes I make."

"That would be my pleasure." He kept smiling, but his voice became serious. "Look, I doubt you called me just to ask for help on your story. What is it that I can do for you?

Julia looked around the restaurant. *Was this a good place to talk about Robert's suspicions and his warnings about activities near her hotel?* The other customers were involved in their own conversations. It looked safe.

She told Carlo about the rumors she said she had heard and the questions they raised. She even mentioned her own uneasiness about the mysterious man outside the hotel. And, after some hesitation, she shared a little of Robert's fears about whatever his police informant had told him was going on in the vacant building near the hotel and about his feeling that she might be in danger.

"So," she concluded. "I guess what I need from you is whether or not you think my friend Robert is right. From what you know of police activities and crime in Florence, is there any reason why I should have to move out of that hotel and into another one? I mean, I really like it there. I don't want to leave if I don't have to."

Carlo took a while to respond. He looked out toward the piazza, deep in thought, obviously trying to decide how much to tell her. And then he looked directly at her.

"There are rumors about trafficking of all kinds in the historic center. I'm not exactly in the know on the specifics, so I can't tell you if it's in the neighborhood of your hotel or even what is imminent. But I can tell you the police are on their guard. The murder near the Duomo seemed to signal that something was coming to a boil. It was done in a way and in a place that was obviously meant to evoke memories of the city's history of political rivalries. They're investigating it pretty carefully."

"That's what Robert told me, too," Julia exclaimed. "But he didn't know—or say—in what way it was related to whatever else was about to happen."

Carlo leaned forward and grabbed her hand as he spoke. "I can't figure out how he would know about this. As far as I know, he isn't any closer to the police than I am, even if he has a source in the department. They keep things like this pretty much to themselves. And if he's not getting this intelligence from the police, where is he getting it?"

Julia stared at him. Had Robert's information come from someone close to those engaged in trafficking? But who? And did Robert have any connection to that kind of crime?

From the stricken look on Julia's face, Carlo knew he had said too much. Why alarm her when police business was often a matter of speculation by people outside the department? And Florence was not crime-free by any means. Surely Julia was aware of that. It was like any big city. Beneath its beautiful exterior lay pockets of corruption, violence, and deceit of all kinds.

"Look," he said gently, his response modulating to a tone that was calm and matter-of-fact. "We don't know definitively that anything is about to happen, or if it is, that it involves your hotel in a way that poses any danger to you. Your friend's story suggests it's only for a few days, possibly affecting a particular part of the hotel—the part where you were staying."

"That's right," Julia said with some relief. "If I just ask for a room in another wing, I might be all right."

"I'll see if I can find out from my sources if anything unusual is expected to happen," he added quickly. "Until then, I think it may be best that you stay where you are. But I'll let you know as soon as I can."

He decided to make the change of venues seem more like an opportunity than an inconvenience. "You know, it would be a shame for you not to be able to explore that other neighborhood more closely. The towers and some of the other sites nearby would be wonderful material for your article."

Julia's face brightened. "The towers, of course!" she

exclaimed. "I had forgotten about them. They would provide a great sidebar to my article. I've been told that one of them used to be a prison."

"For women, yes. Back in the Middle Ages."

"But for what crimes? Why would women be sent to prison?"

"Small crimes, usually. Unpaid debts. Or for refusing to marry the spouses selected for them in an arranged marriage. Being in a separate place was also for their own protection. Women prisoners were sometimes attacked by male prisoners or even their keepers."

"What an awful time to live," Julia said. "For women anyway. I can't even imagine the sadness and fear they must have felt."

"Some did, probably. But you're seeing their plight through your own eyes, from a twentieth-century perspective. Back then, it was just the way things were."

"That may be true. But it's still awful. What you've told me just makes me want to learn more about it." She was smiling again, her eyes bright with images she could see in this new aspect to her project. "And, you know what? I'm going to get started on that this afternoon."

CHAPTER 14

Darkness. Impenetrable at first.
Piero opened his eyes and struggled to pull his scattered thoughts together. "Where am I?" he mumbled, searching for light—any kind of light—in his surroundings. He squinted and began to see patches of gray break through the shadows that enveloped him.

Gradually, a flurry of other sensations began to crowd his consciousness. Cold. Pain. He was lying on a damp, hard surface, his arms twisted somehow behind his back, making his shoulders throb. His neck hurt. And there was an ache in one of his temples. The result of a blow, perhaps. Or maybe it was because his head was resting on a paving stone, a sharp-edged, unyielding pillow.

Not that he had been sleeping. The location was hardly conducive to repose. And now, something was gently stroking his cheek. He rolled over on his back and blinked, bringing his blurred vision more into focus, and found himself gazing into the amber eyes of a curious, jet-black cat. The animal was friendly but a little concerned, maybe even frightened. The fur on its back stood on end, and it placed its forepaws firmly on Piero's chest as it leaned down to lick his face with a rough, wet tongue. Piero groaned, and the cat pulled away, all four paws now firmly planted on the pavement. It cocked its head, still staring at Piero.

Piero smiled despite his circumstance and confused state. "You are a good cat," he muttered and was rewarded with another barrage of cat kisses. "Can you help me out of here?"

He sat up carefully, rubbing his face and his arms to restore some feeling other than pain. Pulling himself up brick by brick on the wall lining the narrow passageway, he rose and stood swaying for a moment, trying to get his bearings and his balance.

The cat looked up at him, still curious. Then it turned, moving away from him, tail swinging from side to side, out of the darkness toward a brightening open space at the end of the passage. Piero followed, staggering a few yards behind. When the two of them emerged into a small piazza, the cat looked back one more time and scampered off into a nearby alley.

Piero was alone, but he felt better in the sunlight that cast a soft glow on him. He kept moving out of the piazza and down another narrow passage until he arrived at a larger street whose small shops and apartments were familiar to him. He was still in the historic core, he realized, not far from the Duomo and the busy life that teemed there, close to the place where he worked and where he could vaguely remember being seized and manhandled. He could go home, he thought. But he wanted company. So, he headed for the hotel, swaying and stumbling. The few people he encountered looked at him warily and stepped aside, giving him room and whispering to each other as he passed by.

Weary and disoriented, he pulled his shoulders back and struggled to maintain his balance. *I must look pretty bad.*

Julia had spent much of the time following her lunch with Carlo doing online research on the towers and their neighborhoods at the university library. In the 11th and 12th centuries, she learned, the towers had been symbols of wealth as well as places of refuge from violence among families whose desire for power was often advanced by conflict and intrigue. That era eventually came to an end, however, as did the flurry of tower-building. Some structures had collapsed because they had been built too high. Others had been knocked down by political opponents. Still more had been shortened after the 13th century, when a decree of the new Florentine republic established that towers should be of the same height. By modern times, only a few were still around, pointing their stony fingers to the sky.

She had decided to photograph the towers near the hotel where she had stayed her first few days in Florence. Its name— *Torrevecchia* (the old tower)—now had greater significance to her. As she stood in the piazza, mentally composing the shots before she took them, a lone figure staggered into view, wearing a wrinkled jacket and a white shirt and slacks that were soiled and torn. Hadn't she seen him before in the hotel? Just a couple of days ago?

"*Signore,*" she called out to him. "Are you all right?"

He turned toward her as he heard her voice, and then, swaying, he collapsed.

When Piero opened his eyes again, he was lying on a padded banquette near the fireplace in the hotel bar. Leaning over him was the young woman who had spoken to him in the piazza. *I've seen her before.* But it was all very hazy for him right now. His thoughts were jumbled and unfocused.

Strangely, his clearest memories were of a black cat, but he didn't remember why. "I hope he's okay," he muttered.

"Who is okay?" the girl asked, leaning forward to hear his faint voice. She moved aside as a man sat down on a chair next to him and flashed a pen light into his eyes.

"He's had a concussion. And there's been some trauma involving his neck. We need to get him to a hospital."

CHAPTER 15

While the bellman was being loaded into an ambulance, Julia stayed for a while to meet with a police officer summoned to investigate the assault. After he had spoken briefly with the injured man, he was meticulously interviewing everyone who had been present when Piero—she had learned that was the bellman's name—had stumbled into the piazza, wounded and incoherent.

A few hotel employees were gathered around the entrance to the bar, sharing chilling details of the attack on their coworker. Julia recognized one of them as the afternoon bartender. "I heard him tell the policeman it happened when he was in the alley next to the hotel. He had seen things there while he was in the roof garden," a woman said in a low voice. Julia gasped. *The roof garden is just down the hall from my room.* She moved closer to hear more of their excited chatter. The bartender waved his hand dismissively. "But he wandered into the piazza today from someplace else. If he was attacked in the alley, where has he been since then and how did he get there?"

Julia drew away from the others, struggling with knowledge of the danger that may have been so close to her. Piero had gone missing after Robert had called and insisted that she move out of her room. *So, he had been right. There was something suspicious nearby.*

Her interview with the policeman—Officer Niccolo Rossi, it said on the card he handed her—focused mainly on her encounter with the bellman in the piazza. It didn't last long. The address and telephone number where he could be reached were in bold letters under his name. He'd be in touch if he needed to talk to her again, he said.

After she left Officer Rossi, she went upstairs to gather her remaining luggage and check out of her room. She told the desk clerk that she would return as soon as she had taken care of other pressing business. The clerk nodded knowingly but doubted that she would come back at all. Not that he would blame her. There had been too much excitement in the vicinity the past few days. No wonder guests were getting a little skittish.

After photographing a few more tower neighborhoods and sites that had been renovated for the Jubilee, Julia was back at her *pensione* on the Lungarno, bags unpacked.

Pensione Europa. A good name for it. Its wrought-iron elevator and second floor entry (a security precaution for all the businesses whose first floor opened on the walkway by the river) were straight out of a movie. The rest of the place was a hotel version of sensible shoes. The practical and plain decor in the wood-paneled dining room was mirrored throughout the building. The no-nonsense emphasis on efficiency in the style and routines of the place created a time warp for everyone and everything in it.

Her room was plain and utilitarian, its space dominated by a sturdy four-poster bed. A love seat and the upholstered chair where she had slept the night before were arranged at angles to each other along one of the side walls. On the opposite wall was the entrance to her bathroom, flanked by a small refrigerator and a side table with a coffee pot, cups and a pair of wine glasses. A large wardrobe with a built-in chest of drawers anchored the end of the room, spacious enough to contain the clothes she had brought with her. She stored her luggage on top of the wardrobe.

Everything was monochrome. Missing were the floral designs that brightened the decor she had enjoyed so much in the *Hotel Torrevecchia*. The only features reminiscent of her room there were the ceiling-high shuttered windows overlooking the street outside the *pensione*. Still, the simplicity of her accommodations didn't bother Julia at all. She was in fact comforted by its practicality.

She particularly enjoyed the homey atmosphere in the hotel dining room. By the time she had finished settling into her room, she was ready for dinner and the chance to relax. Sitting at her table, sipping a glass of Chianti, she toyed with the food she had ordered. The photo essay was the last thing on her mind now.

What were her options? Should she call Carlo to let him know what happened? Robert? Or should she go it alone? There was nothing that suggested she was now personally in danger, and if she had been, she was no longer in the location where she was most at risk. But she didn't feel like keeping this to herself. Why didn't either of them call? Both had said they would be in touch. And both knew where she was. It was all so unsettling.

The other guests having dinner provided a welcome distraction. *Definitely British. Brits like this kind of place.*

While she ate, she discreetly sized up the other guests, assigning identities to them from their resemblance to characters in the British movies and TV series she was fond of back home.

A young couple, obviously honeymooners, held hands across their small table next to a window and gazed into each other's eyes, oblivious to everything and everyone else in the room. Lucy and George from *A Room with a View,* she decided.

An older woman, matronly and Miss Marple-like in her tweed suit, dined in a silence that was interrupted occasionally with mumbled single-word requests of her waiter. Her manner was curt and demanding. From the attention she was getting from the staff, Julia suspected she was a frequent guest.

At another table, to the side of the room, was a young woman, probably in her early twenties, also alone. She was at ease in her isolation, reading a book as she ate, ignoring everyone else in the room. Definitely a *Little Women* type. Jo March?

And who am I? Julia couldn't help but wonder. Did she look as much like someone from central casting as everybody else in the room did?

Smiling as she finished her dessert, she folded her napkin and placed it carefully on the table. It would still be there the next morning, another of the hotel's time-worn practices. Guests sat at the same place and the same table every meal, a convention that made them feel like they were at a home away from home.

As she prepared to return to her room, her waiter approached with a note and handed it to her. She opened it eagerly, the chain of her light-hearted musings broken by a reminder of the problems of her present. But the note wasn't from either Carlo or Robert, the two men she hoped would contact her. It was from the police officer who had interrogated her at the hotel. He was in the lobby. He wanted to ask her a few more questions.

The lobby was a small room to the side of the reception area on the second floor. Officer Rossi was standing outside it, gazing out the window at the river and the Ponte Vecchio. He turned and smiled as he heard Julia approach.

"*Buona sera, signorina.* Do you have a moment for us to talk a little more about what you know of the hotel where Piero Manca was attacked?" He motioned to the lobby, and Julia moved briskly there, taking a seat on the settee opposite the chair the officer had selected.

"I'm sorry to bother you so soon after the disturbing experience you had this afternoon, but I learned after I finished my interview with you that you had been a guest at the *Hotel Torrevecchia*. I was under the impression that you were only passing through the piazza when Piero arrived." His English was impeccable, and Julia couldn't help being charmed by his Florentine accent. Dark haired and dark eyed, he was unaware of the effect of his appearance. *Handsome but humble. I like that.* As he spoke, he took out a small notebook and a pen and began writing.

"Yes, I had a room there," she admitted, "but I have been here since last night."

"And yet the desk clerk at the *Torrevecchia* told me you had checked out only today after the incident with Piero."

"I hadn't completely checked out until then. Some of

my belongings were still in my room there, but this afternoon I decided it made more sense to have everything together in one hotel. So, I packed them up and brought them here."

"I see. Do you mind telling me why you were staying in two hotels at the same time?"

Julia realized how suspicious that might look. Did Officer Rossi think she was implicated in the attack on Piero, or in some of the other activities that Robert claimed were going on in that neighborhood? When she answered, she knew that her voice sounded strained. It was best to level with him. Tell him everything she knew, however ridiculous it might sound.

"I... I was told something about the hotel that frightened me. I decided to move out for a few days until I could find out if it was as unsafe there as I had been told."

"Unsafe in what way?"

She sighed. The story still seemed incredible. "I was told there were some things going on in the neighborhood that might make it dangerous for me to stay in my room."

"What kinds of things?"

"I don't know exactly. Just some sort of criminal activity somewhere close by."

"Who told you that?"

She hesitated. *Should I draw Robert into all this?* And then she thought, *Why not? He's the reason why I did the things that now look very strange to the police.*

She decided to mention Robert without giving too much detail. "A friend of mine told me he thought I should avoid staying in that hotel for a while. He lives in Florence and said he had heard some rumors circulating after the murder in the Duomo."

"I see." Officer Rossi's look was quizzical. "But I still

don't understand. Why didn't you just move out entirely? Why keep some of your belongings in the room if you were afraid to stay there?"

"Because...I know this sounds odd...but because I didn't believe it was necessary. I just thought if I stayed away for a few days if there was some danger, it would be over soon, and I could move back. I liked the hotel. I didn't want to leave, but..."

"But what?"

"After what happened to Piero, I decided maybe there was some truth to what I had been told. That it would be best not to stay there any longer. So, I checked out."

Officer Rossi stared at her just long enough for her to know that he was mentally processing her story. "I understand," he said finally, and smiled. "You know, I assume, that Piero was attacked after he had seen something from the roof garden. That's down the hall from the room I've been told you were occupying."

"I heard that, too, from a couple of the hotel employees while I was waiting to talk to you. It sounded like stories of the attack were already becoming part of the staff rumor mill."

"Didn't you notice anything? Any unusual sounds or activities?"

"No. I wasn't in my room a lot. And I don't know when that happened to him. But I didn't hear anything while I was there."

"And what about elsewhere in the hotel? Did you notice anything strange?"

She stared at him for a moment. *Should I tell him about the strange man I saw my first couple of days in Florence?*

"No," she answered. "The fireplace in the bar made some weird noises, but that's all. Nothing more."

Officer Rossi closed his notebook and put the pen back in his pocket. *Did he believe me?* Julia wondered. And worried. He smiled again. "Thank you for your help. I may be in touch with you again as we continue our investigation. And if you remember anything more—anything you think might add to what you have already told me—please contact me at the number on my card."

He left quickly, and Julia remained for a few moments in the small lobby. Long enough to be there when the ancient hotel elevator ascended from the ground floor and brought Robert to the reception area.

CHAPTER 16

Robert looked bad. His clothes were rumpled. It was obvious he hadn't changed his shirt and slacks since their dinner and hadn't slept much either if the dark circles under his red-rimmed eyes were any indication. He also seemed unusually agitated, pacing back and forth while Julia observed him from her place on the settee.

It wasn't clear if he was upset by the events of the afternoon as she had described them, or by the line of questioning Office Rossi had pursued with her. He kept asking her to repeat what Rossi said and how she had replied. "I just want to get the story straight," he said.

"There's nothing to get straight, Robert. I just told him what had happened and why I had moved out of the hotel. I thought you said you had a connection with someone in the police department. Surely I didn't say anything that Officer Rossi didn't already know about activities in that neighborhood?"

"It's not that he didn't know, it's just that...now someone else knows."

Julia stared at him for a moment. None of this was making any sense. She tried to calm him down by changing the subject.

"I talked to Carlo today, too. You remember him—from the university? We had lunch."

Robert wasn't listening. "I'm going to be gone for a few days," he said abruptly. "I'll call you when I'm back. It sounds like you're going to be pretty busy anyway."

For the first time in their conversation, he looked at her with concern. "Are you going to be okay?"

"Of course I am. Are you okay?" She knew she was going to miss him, and she was worried about the way he looked and the way he was acting.

"Sure. I just have to get some things taken care of. I'll explain later. You just have to keep trusting me."

"I do, Robert," she said. But she wasn't sure she meant it.

He kissed her on the cheek and left quickly. Back in her room for the evening, she went over their conversation again and again in her mind. *Why was it so unnerving? Do I really trust him?*

Julia's telephone conversation with Carlo the next morning went much better. He called her just after she finished breakfast. He had read a small item in the paper about the assault on the hotel bellman. The article didn't mention Piero's name. Just a short blurb with a "man attacked in historic center of Florence" angle that didn't divulge many particulars.

"I recognized the hotel as the one where you had been staying," Carlo said. "Were you aware this happened?"

When Julia explained to him about her presence in the

piazza when Piero arrived, and the interrogations by Office Rossi, Carlo first expressed alarm about her involvement in the situation and then relief at the fact that the police were so quick and thorough in their response to it.

"It sounds like it's being handled well. I know Rossi. He's a good man. He was a student of mine at the university for a while before he decided he wanted a career in police work. He'll get to the bottom of whatever is going on. And if you were under suspicion, you'd know it by now. I wouldn't worry."

"Did you find out anything that suggested this attack could be related to the rumors Robert heard about criminal activities in the neighborhood?"

"No, I haven't turned up anything. But you were wise to move out of the hotel. Just as a precaution. If there is anything going on—and I don't know what it is—you're safer where you are now."

Their conversation ended with a promise from Carlo that he would be in touch if he found out anything she needed to know.

CHAPTER 17

Nic Rossi wasn't used to thinking about anything other than his work. It had been so long since there had been a woman in his life that he had lost the ability to feel an attraction. Or so he thought. But he couldn't stop thinking about the woman at the hotel—*Julia. Wasn't that her name?*

There was something about her that appealed to him. *Independent but somehow vulnerable. Just like Maria.*

He shuffled through the papers on his desk, trying to concentrate on the cases he was reviewing. The attack on Piero Manca was one of them. A police squad had searched the building where Piero claimed he had seen some suspicious activities, but it was empty. No evidence of any previous occupants. That didn't mean there hadn't been something going on there. Nic and his team knew that. The syndicates were very good at covering their traces. The police would continue to keep an eye on the building and on others close by.

Luca, a senior officer and one of his best friends, entered the office and sat down in the chair across the desk from him. They had talked a lot about the investigation. Were there any leads they had missed?

"How about the woman who was in the piazza when Piero came back to the hotel?" he asked, trying to sound nonchalant.

Luca looked surprised. "You've interrogated her twice and seemed to accept what she told you." His left eyebrow arched upward, always a sign that he doubted something he had just heard. "Are you sure your interest in her is only because of the Piero Manca case?"

"What do you mean? I wasn't suggesting she is a suspect." He stopped to clear his throat and adjust his tie. "I'm just thinking maybe I missed something. Talking to her again might clear that up."

Luca was quiet. He looked at Nic and smiled. "Maybe you want an excuse to see her again." He chuckled. He tipped his head and crossed his arms. "Why don't you admit you're attracted to her? If you are, you should ask her out."

"You know very well why I won't ask her out—or any other woman."

"Maria?"

"Yes."

Luca leaned forward. "Nic, you've been incredibly faithful to Maria. But we have no idea where she is or what happened to her. And you're still pretty young. And lonely. You should allow yourself to have some fun."

Unthinkable. I won't betray her. I will honor my vows.

Nic glared at Luca. "Listen, this woman may have someone else in her life anyway. I'm pretty sure she's the one Robert told me about when he found out she was coming to Florence."

"If she's seeing Robert, she'll refuse to go out with you. And if she's not—it doesn't hurt to ask."

"There's still Maria,"

Luca rose from his chair and headed for the door. Another familiar gesture. A sign of impatience.

"I'm not talking about a long-term relationship, Nic. She's a tourist. She'll be back in the US in a few weeks or months. You might as well enjoy her company until she leaves. That's not being disloyal to Maria."

He walked out of the office and slammed the door behind him.

He's right. I am lonely. Maybe it wouldn't hurt just to see her again.

CHAPTER 18

Julia was on her own now. No Robert, wherever he was. Carlo was available if needed. But somehow, she felt liberated, free to concentrate on her work and her professional reason for being in Florence. Although her neighborhood was open to traffic and passersby on the Lungarno, there had been no more encounters with the man whose behavior had frightened her so much when she had seen him outside the *Torrevecchia* and in the Duomo.

She settled comfortably into the life and accommodations in the *pensione* that was now her home, funky as it was. Everyone on the staff was friendly and helpful. And over dinner, she began to enjoy extended conversations with several of the other guests.

She had even won over the woman in the tweed suit, who had originally struck her as aloof and difficult but turned out to be very accommodating and helpful. "Call me Amanda," the woman had said when they first began to chat with each other. A retired travel agent who now spent every summer on her own in Tuscany, she happily shared with Julia her extensive knowledge about Florence —including the history of its towers.

One detail was particularly intriguing to Julia. "Did you know that, in earlier eras, some towers anchored entire city blocks?" Amanda told her. "They were parts of complexes that were actually closed communities tied together by balconies and wooden walkways above street level."

"So the towers didn't stand alone?" Julia asked. "I wonder if any of those connections between buildings still exist, either on the inside or the outside of the towers?"

"Not that I know of. At least not exterior connections. I've never seen any."

With plenty of time to concentrate on her photo essay project, Julia visited venues she had carefully identified in her research. Her days were occupied with searching out a variety of churches and monuments in the historic center of the city and photographing them from every angle, both inside and out, whenever possible. She had also captured images of people who frequented them, especially among the increasing numbers of tourists visiting the city. For her personal story, she sought a few locations just for the memories they brought back.

Slowly, the intrigue surrounding the *Hotel Torrevecchia* had faded from her consciousness. Carlo had discovered no new information, so he stopped calling. And Robert had not tried to reach her at all. That was fine with her, she decided. This was a business trip. Any possibility that it would become anything else had faded.

Her evenings were spent adding the text accompanying the photo layout that she began to construct on her computer every night after dinner. It was all coming together nicely. The personal reminiscences from both her childhood and her life with Bill had become more comfortable--stories that she enjoyed attaching to the scenes of the city that she was coming to love once again. Her return was providing a renewal of its own. She was capturing everything in notebook entries that now focused entirely on descriptions of scenes for her magazine assignment.

A week after the attack on Pierre Manca, Officer Rossi called the *pensione* and left a message for her at the reception desk, indicating he would like to talk to her again. The contact from him brought back darker memories.

He announced his arrival at the *pensione* the same way he had the first time he had come to visit: a waiter delivered a note to her table just as she was finishing dinner. She found the policeman in the lobby again, but this time, he wasn't in business attire. He was in slacks, an open-collared white shirt and a blazer, casual but fashionable.

"What can I help you with, Officer Rossi?" she asked, a bit nervously. *Am I under suspicion?*

"I'm not here about the attack on Piero Manca," he said. "That investigation is moving along nicely. And we don't need anything more from you." He hesitated, looking a little uncertain about what to say next.

"So....why are you here?" Julia asked. The minute she said it, she realized how impertinent it must sound. She smiled, hoping that softened her response a bit.

He smiled back. "First, you don't need to call me Officer Rossi. My name is Niccolo. Nic. And I'm here to...ask you out...if you're interested. There's a wine bar near here. Would you like to join me for a drink?"

Stunned for a moment by an invitation she hadn't expected, Julia assessed Officer Rossi in the new light the situation presented. *I have no social life at all in Florence, and he's attractive in a way that doesn't remind me of either Bill or Robert. That's good.*

He appeared to be about her age. Hadn't Carlo said he had been one of his students? They'd have that to talk about, not just the awful mess with Piero.

She thought for a moment and realized how much she was missing nights out in her beautiful Florence. *Why not?*

"Yes. I would love that," she said.

CHAPTER 19

Journal

Not much going on. Just work. The project is turning out well. Haven't heard anything from Robert or Carlo. Nothing more about whatever is supposedly going to happen near my old hotel.

But I just had an amazing evening. Officer Rossi—the one investigating the attack on that poor bellman the other day—stopped by and asked me out for a drink. We went to a charming wine bar close by. Lots of locals as well as tourists, as best I could tell. He is a fascinating guy, not what I would have expected. He knew Carlo, said he had been a student at the university. Must have been close to the time when Bill and I were there, but somehow our paths never crossed. Different majors, different routines, I guess. Anyway, he plans to return to school someday. Wants to become a lawyer, but loves police work now. Says he enjoys the mysteries that he sometimes has to solve. Like the one he is working on now. He wouldn't say much about the case, of course, but I gather there may be more to the story about why Piero was attacked than I realized at first. Makes me *glad to be safe in my new location. Just too much unrest in the streets near the Duomo.*

He asked me out again. Going to the opera on the weekend.

Their first outings were very open and casual. An evening at the opera, then a couple more at small concerts in local churches. Sometimes, they simply enjoyed a long, leisurely meal at one of the restaurants in central Florence. Their conversations, cautious and impersonal at first, slowly became more candid and revealing.

"You were a student of Carlo's at the same time I was at the university. Right?" Julia asked over dinner early in their time together.

"Yes. In Political Science."

"But I don't recall seeing you at any of the social gatherings and parties where students liked to get together on weekends. Carlo used to come to them, too."

"No. I was married at the time. My wife didn't like those groups. She felt awkward."

Married? Julia was surprised by that revelation. But Nic seemed willing to talk, so she pursued the point.

"Awkward? Why?"

"Because she—Maria—hadn't attended the university. Wasn't interested. She worked as a waitress at a nightclub in the city center and was more comfortable with that life. That's where I met her. She was pretty young—still a teenager when I married her."

"But...the marriage didn't last?" Julia immediately knew that was the wrong thing to ask. Nic gulped, put his wine glass down abruptly and stared for a long time at his plate.

"It didn't last because Maria disappeared," he said

finally, slowly, picking his words carefully as if it hurt to use them. "The police thought she was abducted while coming home from work one night. Maybe murdered. I was at the library, studying."

Julia felt awful. She didn't know what to say or do. *Should I change the subject? Wait to let him speak?*

Nic broke the silence. "That's when I dropped out of the university and joined the police force. I wanted to find out what happened to her. I wanted to get whoever was responsible. Make sure they were punished."

"And did you?" Her question was little more than a whisper.

"No. It's an unsolved case. I wouldn't have been allowed to work on it anyway because of my personal involvement. But that's why I like to be assigned to investigations of crimes in the neighborhoods around the Duomo. I keep hoping that sometime, somehow, there will be a connection—that I'll find out what happened to her in the process of investigating something that at first doesn't seem related…."

His voice trailed off as he looked up at Julia.

"You're the first woman I have dated seriously since then."

"Because I remind you of her?"

"No. Because you don't remind me of her. Does that make sense?"

Julia remembered her initial reaction to Nic. Relief that he was unlike either Bill or Robert. Her failed romance with Bill now seemed trivial by comparison with Nic's loss.

"Yes, I know exactly what you mean." She smiled and reached out to touch his hand.

He squeezed hers in return.

. . .

After that, the more time they spent together, the more they shared. He was an amateur musician who played backup keyboard in local clubs whenever he had the time and opportunity. That wasn't very often these days. The life of a policeman was too full, the hours too unpredictable. And he loved the art of the Italian Renaissance, as she did. That led to several visits to the Uffizi, where they compared notes on their favorite paintings and salons.

After an afternoon excursion on one of his days off, they stopped at Paoli for dinner. In contrast to her evening there with Robert, she and Nic had little interest in the surroundings or the other guests. They chose a table away from the entrance and sat close to each other against the thick side wall, ignoring the bustling night-time activity of the restaurant. He ordered an exquisite *Brunello*, carefully pouring each of them a glass before raising his in a toast.

"To my beautiful Julia. And to us."

As they touched glasses, his gaze was tender and affectionate. Was their relationship moving too fast? They had been dating for only a couple of weeks, but they had seen each other almost every night. This occasion had an intensity that hadn't been there before.

After they finished their desserts and Nic had settled the check, he put his arm around her. Stirrings that she hadn't felt since her break-up with Bill made her shift uncomfortably. He noticed. He put his hand on her thigh, resting it there at first and then moving slowly to the inside of her leg. She turned to him as he leaned toward her and pressed his lips against hers, gently at first, and then harder.

Nic whispered in her ear. "Let's go." He stood up, grabbed her hand, and led her out of the restaurant.

They hurried back to her *pensione* and waited impatiently while the elevator transported them to her floor. Julia hadn't felt this nervous since she was in college. After fumbling for her key, with a trembling hand, she inserted it into the lock and flung open the door to her room.

Once inside, Nic pulled her close and helped her remove her clothes, dropping them gently on the floor. She wrapped her arms around his neck, and they kissed as he slowly undressed, and then she drew him over to the bed. She threw the comforter aside and lay down, pulling him on top of her.

It had been a long time since either of them had been with anyone. "I love you," Nic said afterward as they lay curled together, bathed in the moonlight shining through the shutters in the window near the bed.

"I love you, too," she said. "I do."

CHAPTER 20

Florence felt like home now. The original purpose guiding Julia's return had brought her to a place of trust and belonging, largely because Nic's presence in her life gave her a personal confidence she hadn't known before. Rarely with Robert. Not with Bill.

There were moments when she felt guilty about not missing Robert and worried about his absence. She hadn't seen him for well over a month now. It seemed past the point when they could have gotten together again.

Her plans had changed, of course, although he didn't know that. She had mailed her photo essay to the magazine and was waiting for the editor's response. The hardest part had been turning her notebook entries into text to accompany the photos—her personal reflections on the assignment that had brought her back to Florence. She had wanted to convey a sense of nostalgia about her connections with the city in the past, but she struggled to recapture it now that she was so absorbed by her life with Nic.

She had decided she wouldn't leave Florence until she knew that the magazine didn't want any revisions in her article. As the tourist season became busier, arrangements for another stay would be much more complicated and expensive than simply canceling her plans elsewhere and staying in Florence to redo shots, add images of vacationers as more of them came to Italy, or rewrite her description of the experiences that had once meant so much to her. At least, that was the rationale she had come up with to justify extending her stay. The magazine was willing to cover her expenses if she found aspects of the millennium and the Jubilee that she could turn into sidebars or even separate articles. They had also responded favorably to a couple of other stories she had proposed about restaurants and entertainment activities in Florence.

But the reality was that she didn't want to take the chance of losing Nic just as their affair was beginning to grow more serious. He had asked her to move into his apartment. Despite the yearning she felt for him, she was reluctant. It was a big step in their relationship, and she wasn't sure she was ready to take it.

For the time being, she kept her room in *Pensione Europa*, enjoying the freedom of exploring Florence by herself during the daytime, and spending nights with Nic when he wasn't on assignment.

Carlo was in touch occasionally, but for a while it was simply to tell her that he hadn't found much to report. Then, unexpectedly, he called one day and suggested they meet for lunch in a relaxed setting where they could exchange news and relax.

As before, she found him sitting outside the trattoria near the Pitti Palace. She was late—or maybe he was early again—but it didn't matter. She settled comfortably at their table, and Carlo smiled.

"You look very happy," he said.

"I am," she said. She could feel herself blushing, so she stared intently at the menu, trying to avoid his gaze.

"Well, you must have been doing something a lot more fun than just working on that photo essay," he teased. She laughed. "Seriously," he added, "if you've found someone who brings you so much joy, I think that's wonderful."

She nodded. "I have. I haven't felt this at peace with my life in...I don't know...years, I think. I guess it shows."

"I don't want to be nosy, but is Nic the new man in your life?" he asked.

"Yes. We've been dating for about a month. I guess April is a good time for romance." She laughed adding, "We actually have quite a bit in common."

"He's a good soul. I'm glad you found each other," he said. He smiled again, and then he became solemn. "I hate to change the subject, but—have you heard from Robert lately?" he asked.

Julia felt a rush of guilt. She had been so wrapped up in her work and her developing romance with Nic that she hadn't called Carlo to tell him any of her worries about Robert. "No. The last time I saw him, he said he had something he had to get worked out and he'd get back to me in a few days. I haven't heard from him since."

Carlo was quiet for a few moments. He looked around to make sure no one in the restaurant was listening and leaned forward. "I think he may be in danger."

"Danger? How?"

"Well, after you and I last talked, I asked some of the folks I know in the police department if they knew him.

I've been told there is one detective who is acquainted with him—they didn't say who—but Robert hasn't been in touch with him for a few weeks, which is unusual. He seems to be missing."

"Oh, dear God!" she exclaimed. "Do they have any suspicions about what may have happened to him?"

"I gather he has been interested in—almost obsessed with—whatever has been going on in or around the neighborhood near the hotel where you used to be staying. He told the detective he was going to do a little investigating on his own. The detective tried to talk him out of that, of course. But that was the last that the police have seen of him."

The waiter arriving with their meals interrupted their conversation, after which they ate in silence for a few minutes. Julia picked at her food until, finally, she couldn't hold back her feelings. "So, what are we going to do? If Robert is in some sort of trouble, I want to help him if I can."

"Julia, I don't think there is anything we can do. I'm sure the detective or someone in the department is looking into the matter. And I doubt they want us getting in the way. If they need something from us, they'll ask."

"But are they aware that I might have some useful information about Robert?"

"Yes, I told them about you. If they're interested, they'll be in touch. But they may not want you to become too involved. It's a dangerous situation, Julia. You could get hurt. Let the police handle it."

"If you didn't want me to get involved, why did you tell me? It doesn't feel right to me not to try to do something, at least."

"Julia, I didn't want to make you upset. I just thought I

should tell you what I had heard." He paused. "It would be different, maybe, if somebody in the police department would reveal more about what is going on."

Julia leaned back in her chair, relieved. "I get what you're suggesting. I'll ask him."

CHAPTER 21

Nic was looking forward to another dinner with Julia. At Paoli, of course. Their special place. He arrived early, eager to see her after a long day at work, and took a seat at their favorite table along the wall. He motioned to the waiter who was stationed close by. He looked familiar. "We'll have a bottle of wine."

"The usual?" the waiter smiled.

"Yes," Nic said and chuckled. *I guess we're regulars here now.*

The waiter brought a bottle of *Brunello* and poured a glass for him. Sipping it slowly, he thought about the problems that had arisen in the investigation of the attack on Piero Manca. The case was going nowhere even though he and his team had followed up every lead they had. Unfortunately, there weren't many. *It happened in a public place. Why haven't more people come forward?*

He leaned back against the brick wall and closed his eyes. His thoughts turned to his unfolding relationship with Julia. *Luca was right. I did need someone in my life. I'm so lucky I met her.*

But were things getting too complicated between them? He wanted her, needed her. And yet, realistically, what could the future hold? Maria would always be in his heart.

Julia arrived a few minutes late, dressed in a fashionable pantsuit. She leaned forward to kiss him on the cheek before taking her place on the cushioned seat alongside him. *She looks incredible.* He beamed and kissed her back. "I've already ordered the veal and pasta dinner you like so much."

She smiled. "Thanks. That is definitely my favorite meal here."

Over dinner, she shared some stories about her life in the pensione. He couldn't help but laugh. "Typical British tourists," he said.

Then she told him about her conversation with Carlo. "Is it true what he said about Robert? That he has disappeared?" she asked casually as she twirled a helping of spaghetti carbonara on her fork. They had not talked about Robert before.

"Of course, I know about his disappearance," Nic said. "We're concerned about it because it could be connected to the assault on Piero Manca. And maybe to the attack in front of the Duomo a few weeks ago."

"So why didn't you mention all this to me?"

"Why should I? It's a police matter. I didn't tell you—I can't tell you—about the cases I'm working on. And why is this one so important to you?"

"Because Robert is my friend. I want to help if I can."

"Friend? As in boyfriend?" *So there was something going on between them!*

"No, not a boyfriend. But we've known each other since college. When I came to Florence earlier this spring, he even helped me get started on my magazine assignment. I just feel I've let him down."

"How? Because he warned you about staying in the *Torrevecchia?* He was right about that. But when did you let him down?"

"He came to see me after that, where I'm staying now. He looked bad. Said he would get back to me in a few days, but he didn't. And I didn't try to find out where he was because that was when you and I started seeing each other. I forgot about him. And I shouldn't have."

Nic felt calm again. "Julia, if you want, you can just tell me what you remember of that conversation, and I'll follow up on it. If I find anything that is safe to tell you, I'll let you know."

"Safe?"

He reached out to hold her hand. "You're asking about police business, Julia. I can't say any more than that. I just don't want any harm to come to you."

Julia was surprised at Nic's behavior. It was so unlike his usual way of treating her—more like Bill had been. "Why are you being so protective?" she bristled. "If you can't tell me anything, I'm going to ask around and check out a few places where Robert may have gone."

"Julia, please don't. I lost someone I loved, deeply, because I wasn't there for her. I took her safety for granted. I'm not going to make the same mistake with you. I promise I'll let you know if I learn anything." He raised her hand to his lips. And then he changed the subject. As far as he was concerned, the matter was closed.

But it wasn't for Julia.

CHAPTER 22

Piero was glad to be back on the job. His injuries had healed, but his supervisors at the hotel remained concerned. The police investigation hadn't ruled out the possibility that he was the only target of whoever had assaulted him. The theory seemed to be that he was attacked because he had been too curious about things he had seen from the roof garden, and someone had intended mainly to scare him off. At the same time, the police were tight-lipped about whatever had been going on in the building next door. They had searched the place but found it empty. It appeared just to be a vacant warehouse.

The hotel staff was put on alert, and Piero, in particular, was told to be very cautious while he was on duty. He no longer worked as a bellman because he would be in too much contact with everyone coming into the hotel, and he might have to venture alone into distant parts of the building. His new assignment was as the daytime bartender, which suited him just fine. He liked talking to guests. They enjoyed his banter while they lingered over drinks, and the bar itself had a soothing, comfortable feel.

The first customer of the afternoon was a young woman. *She looks vaguely familiar, although I can't remember where I've seen her before.*

She took her seat at a table next to the fireplace in the old tower and was staring at it intently when he approached.

"May I bring you a drink, *signorina*?"

Distracted, the woman mumbled, *"Pinot grigio."*

When he brought her glass of wine, she regarded him with a look of recognition. "Aren't you the man who was attacked near the hotel?"

Piero was instantly on guard, but he answered anyway. "Yes, but how did you know that?"

"I saw you when you came into the courtyard and collapsed. I helped bring you into the hotel."

Ah yes, now I remember her.

"Your name is Piero, isn't it? I'm glad to see that you are better now."

"I am, yes. Thank you. But I don't recall much about that day or what happened to me before then."

"Haven't the police talked to you about it?"

"Yes, but I can't tell them much. I was knocked unconscious and didn't wake up until just before I found my way back to the hotel. Everything leading up to that is a blur. I had a concussion."

"I heard you were attacked after you were in the roof garden. That was just down the hall from my room."

"You're staying in the hotel?"

"No, I moved to another place after the attacks on you. Too much excitement for me," she said with a slight smile.

Piero nodded. "I don't blame you. But what brings you here today?"

She hesitated before answering. "I'm looking for a friend who has gone missing. I've been going back to all the places I can think of where people might have seen him. This is one of those places. He met with me here."

Her brief description of Robert didn't remind Piero of anyone he had seen. "I'll watch for him," he said. "And if he comes back to the hotel, I'll let him know you are looking for him."

As he started to move away, the woman called out to him. "Did you hear that?"

"Hear what?" He walked back to her table.

"Listen. There's something coming from over there."

They were both quiet. An echo emanated from somewhere close to them, seemingly from the fireplace.

"It could be the wind," Piero suggested.

She stared at the tower and shook her head slowly. "Maybe. But I don't think so."

CHAPTER 23

The sound Julia and Piero had heard, and all that had been going on in the vicinity of the *Hotel Torrevecchia*, triggered a hunch about what had happened to Robert. After she finished dinner back at her *pensione*, with Nic on duty and busy at the police station for the night, she had the evening free for her own explorations.

It was after 10 o'clock, and she knew how foolish it was to venture after dark into areas of the city that Nic, Robert, and Carlo had all said might be dangerous. She was afraid, but she knew there was only one way she could find the answer to the question that remained in her mind.

Striding through the entrance of her former hotel, she glanced over at the front desk, hoping no one would notice her. She was in luck. The receptionist was busy checking in a man whose several pieces of luggage cluttered the lobby, so she headed straight for the elevator and punched the button that took her to the floor where she had once stayed. Walking down the corridor, she entered the roof garden.

In the dark, all she could see were the shadowy shapes of the patio furniture in the middle of the terrace. Hovering over the nearby rooftops was the Duomo, radiant in the glow of the nighttime sky. She walked over to the garden wall and glanced across at the roof of the mysterious building next door. There were no lights in it. No sign of life anywhere in the darkened windows below. She peered over the wall at the alley several floors below.

Could Robert have been there? Trapped somehow by whoever or whatever it was he had set out to investigate? She dismissed the thought. *The police have searched the place already. If there were traces of anything or anyone there, they would have found them by now.*

Moving away from the garden wall, she settled on one of the patio chairs, looked up at the sky, and then over at the vacant building. If, like other towers in Florence, the towers in this neighborhood were parts of complexes linking them to other structures, where were the connections? There weren't any obvious exterior walkways or balconies linking them.

And then it came to her. *The connections might be on the inside.* Maybe in basements or through other less visible entries.

It was an idea worth exploring, but better done in the daytime, when everything was more accessible. For now, however eager she was to investigate further, she knew it was time to return to the safety of her *pensione*.

She left the roof garden and took the elevator down to the lobby. It was crowded now with the people and luggage of a late-arriving tour group. She slipped out the front door and into the nighttime quiet of the piazza and its surrounding streets. Evening activities were drawing to a close. Some of the shops were locked tight. Even the busy, touristy restaurants were wrapping up service to the customers who lingered over drinks after dinner.

Lost in thought about tower complexes and how she might find out more about their interior connections, she turned down a narrow passageway that she knew would take her more directly to the *Pensione Europa*. It was a shortcut she had taken frequently but never this late in the evening. At this time of night, it was silent and deserted. Worried, she quickened her pace to move more rapidly out of the darkened passageway. Her fear intensified when she heard footsteps behind her, matching their pace with hers. She began to walk faster. The footsteps following her moved faster, too.

She started to run, stumbling at first on the uneven pavement and then breaking for the lighted space she could see at the end of the alley. As she neared the open area that loomed ahead of her, she sensed someone immediately behind her and felt a hand grab her arm, pulling her back and throwing her against the rough stone of a building. A sharp pain shot through her shoulder while her knee took the brunt of her impact with the wall. It all happened so quickly, her instinct was simply to reach out for something to keep her from falling. Somehow she found the wrought iron trim of a street-level window and grabbed onto it. Steadying herself, she turned and looked at the person who had attacked her and gasped. "It's you! What do you want from me?"

The man she had seen outside the window of her room in *Hotel Torrevecchia* stood scowling at her and thrust his fist close to her face. "This time, it's just to give you a warning. Next time, it could be much worse."

"Who are you?"

"It doesn't matter who I am. Just listen to me. Don't get

mixed up with what's going on near that hotel. Stay as far away from there as you can. Or you could get hurt."

He shoved her again as if punctuating his threat, and then he turned and ran back through the passageway and into the darkness. Julia stood for a moment, shaken, and rubbed her shoulder. When she felt able to move again, she hobbled out into the piazza. It would provide a safer and more open route back to her hotel.

As she approached the Lungarno, her emotions alternated between anxiety and confusion, but by the time she reached her *pensione*, they had a sharper focus. She was angry. *What was the man trying to keep her from finding out by frightening her?*

Her knee was more badly scraped than she had realized at first and her shoulder had begun to throb, so she exited the elevator at the second-floor reception area, hoping the hotel would have some first aid supplies there.

No one was at the desk. Not unusual for that time of night, but she really did need to find someone who could at least supply her with bandages and an ice pack. She peeked into the sitting area of the lobby. Amanda was there, her legs curled beneath her on the settee, reading a book. She glanced up as Julia entered the room and smiled. "Well, you've been out late. What have you been...?"

She stopped when she saw Julia's bleeding knee. "Good gracious, what happened to you?" She pulled herself into a sitting position and got up, moving over to where Julia stood.

"I had a little run-in with a wall," Julia said. She didn't feel like revealing how frightening the experience had been. "But I'll be okay if I can just take care of my knee and my shoulder. Do you know where the first aid supplies are?"

Amanda had stayed at the hotel so many times that she knew where everything was. She rummaged briefly in a bottom drawer of the reception desk and produced a box of band-aids, a tube of medicinal cream, and an ice pack.

"Let's go to your room so we can wash off that knee and I can take care of your shoulder. And then I want you to tell me how you got hurt. Seriously."

It didn't take long for Amanda to take care of her injuries. Apparently, earlier in her life, she had some first aid training, a useful skill as it turned out for a tour guide. Once the bleeding on her knee was stopped, Julia could see it was bruised. Her shoulder was a different story. The man had wrenched and twisted it. She tested the extent of the injury by rotating her arm back and forth and felt twinges of pain, but nothing too serious. Probably a slight strain. As far as she could tell, she had no major injuries.

Amanda settled onto the love seat at the side of the room and listened as Julia, propped up against the pillows on her bed, described her trip to the *Torrevecchia* and her encounter with the man in the passageway.

"So why were you over at your other hotel, sneaking around the premises?" Amanda asked.

"I wasn't sneaking around," Julia replied sharply. "I simply went to check something out on the roof garden in the area of the hotel where I had stayed before."

"But you were trying not to be noticed, weren't you?"

"Well, yeah, but...oh, all right, I guess I was sneaking in a way. But I had a legitimate reason for being there."

"Which was...what?"

Julia needed to share her concerns and her suspicions with someone besides Nic. He wouldn't be pleased with her desire to search for Robert on her own, and she had talked enough with Amanda that she felt safe with her. Something about the woman's unflappable approach to everything made her seem trustworthy. So Julia shared Robert's suspicions about mysterious and dangerous activities in the building next to the hotel, described the noises she had heard in the hotel bar and the way Robert had gone missing, and how she thought maybe the towers tied everything together.

Amanda just sat and listened, nodding occasionally. After Julia finished with her account of the attack in the passageway, Amanda sighed, "You may very well be right that the goings-on in that building have something to do with Robert's disappearance, but why do you think the police haven't already looked into the connection?"

"I think they have. But they still haven't found Robert. They may not be considering all the possibilities."

"Such as?"

"The towers. And the fact that they may contain hidden places where he is being held captive."

"Surely you don't believe that?"

"I know it sounds far out, Amanda, but it's the only explanation I can think of. Robert wouldn't simply vanish, especially after he told me he would be back in touch."

"So, what do you plan to do next?" Amanda asked, leaning forward to watch Julia's reaction.

"I'm going to keep looking for Robert. And try to find out more about the construction of the towers near the *Torrevecchia*. There must be a record somewhere—in the library, at the university, maybe."

"And you're going to do this on your own, even after you were attacked and told to keep out of the investigation?"

"Yes. I don't know who else I can ask."

"How about me?" Amanda sat back and smiled.

"You?"

"Why not me?" Amanda answered. "I know the history of buildings in the historic areas of Florence. And I know who to ask about secret entries and hidden passages there. You'll just be wasting your time trying to find that information quickly in a library."

"But what about if we get into trouble, where we are in some sort of danger? You're no stronger than I am. Two women trying to fight off attacks?" The encounter with the man in the passageway was beginning to weigh on Julia.

"Ah, but you see, that's my other value to you. I intend to do everything to make sure we don't do anything that puts us in danger."

Julia thought about her offer for a few seconds. "All right! Let's do it!"

They agreed to meet again over breakfast in the dining room of the *pensione*. "We both need our rest before we start to plan our next steps," Amanda said. "You in particular. You've had a difficult day."

The next morning, Amanda was sitting at her table, studying a dog-eared edition of a guidebook and writing on a notepad in front of her. She looked up as Julia approached and took off the horn-rimmed reading glasses that were perched at the end of her nose. "Good morning," she said, smiling. "How are you feeling?"

"A little stiff and sore, but I'll survive," Julia answered as she eased herself into the chair opposite Amanda. "I see you're already at work. Have you found anything that might be helpful?"

"I've just confirmed my impression of that neighborhood. There were lots of towers there at one time. A few remnants have been incorporated into more modern structures."

"So maybe they are connected to the one in the *Hotel Torrevecchia?* And maybe Robert--or someone--is being held captive there?"

"Slow down. All I said was there had been lots of towers in that vicinity, and parts of them are still there. I don't know if they were connected, but it's not likely they still are."

"What makes you so sure?"

"Because the whole area has been extensively renovated. There's no need for the connections between buildings now. Those were for defense or for easy transit between buildings in times of trouble. They'd be centuries old by now. And no longer necessary or desirable but too costly to eliminate. Some still hold them dear as pieces of the past."

"But what about the noises coming from the tower in the bar? Was that just my imagination?"

"I think that's worth investigating. We can start by finding out if anywhere in the vicinity there's anything left from the tower where the women's prison was located. I know some people close to those projects. I'll just ask them about it."

Julia was quiet, thinking through other possibilities. "Can you also ask someone about any remaining connections to other towers in the area? And can you get us access to any of those buildings—especially their basements—so we can see for ourselves?"

"Maybe. It's worth a try."

"Then that's where we'll start."

CHAPTER 24

Robert took the lead as his team moved quietly along the narrow streets leading to the neighborhood that was their target. Four of them had volunteered to search a section of the city where a particular kind of crime was concentrated.

Sex trafficking, he had learned, was an organized and lucrative illegal activity in the historic core. Cruel, ruthless, and exploitative.

His research, which he shared with others in the group, revealed how widespread the racket was and how it operated. Networks of organized crime sought out young women who were alone and helpless in the city. Most often, the victims were migrants displaced either from their homes in Italy or from other countries—usually Africa or Eastern Europe. Many had left their homelands to escape war or persecution. Others had been sold into slavery by families desperate for the income they could send home. Whatever their origins, they were vulnerable to the promise of help and love from men who took them in, ostensibly at first to provide support and protection and eventually to force them into lives as prostitutes, dependent on their keepers for shelter and food. Without knowing where they could turn to or who they could trust, poor and unskilled in any other way of making a living, they knew no way of escaping from the trap they had fallen into.

The specifics of sex trafficking locations were largely unknown to most of the businesses and centers of culture that brought so many visitors to Florence. It had taken Robert several weeks to find where women were held captive, drawing on the information he had gleaned from conversations with a new informant he had cultivated and from his own late-night excursions into parts of the city where he suspected traffickers operated. The police were aware of prostitution in the city, his source had told him, but they hadn't been able to get a similar sense of the extent of the illegal sex trade, and the crime rings running it.

More likely they weren't interested enough to track down the criminals responsible. His cynicism was fueled by the indifference he had encountered among some of the businessmen with whom he had discussed the need for action. *Were some of them secretly profiting from the exploitation of so many helpless women?* Because of his investigations and his doubts about the effectiveness of local law enforcement, he convinced other members of the group that they needed to expose the criminals and their crimes, and if possible, free the women they victimized. "We need to act fast," he had told them. "Or all my leads will dry up."

Robert and his companions were an advance party charged with striking at the easiest target first. It was a building where, Robert had learned, sex slaves—younger than 18 mainly—were held captive. Their "clients" were brought there by the men who had lured them into their servitude.

The foursome found the entry hidden from view in a darkened alleyway. Robert's informant had assured them that, at this hour, there wouldn't be any activity. The young women would be alone, sleeping. Probably drugged. It would be difficult to help more than a few to escape. If there was a guard on duty, the members of Robert's team were ready to fight. Young, athletic, and strong, they would be able to hold their own if hand-to-hand combat was required.

The entrance to the building was unlocked. Robert looked at the others in surprise. "That doesn't seem right," he whispered.

Sandro, the tallest of the team, whispered back. "Keeping clients out wouldn't be good business. The security is probably upstairs to keep the girls from escaping. Just keep in mind what we've been told about how to get through it."

Robert remained uneasy, but he quietly opened the door, and the team stepped inside, taking a moment to get their bearings. A staircase at the back of the room looked like the only way to the living quarters upstairs. Giuseppe, the huskiest and most adept street fighter among them, took the lead, climbing up toward the floor where, they had been told, the trafficking victims were kept.

At the top of the stairs, another door stood in their way. Giuseppe turned the knob and looked back at his companions, his brow furrowed. This one was unlocked, too. Hesitating a moment, he pushed it open and guided the others inside into an unfurnished space. At the back, they glimpsed a corridor where presumably the young women would be found in their rooms.

Suddenly, from all sides, several men dressed in black and swinging cudgels rushed forward. Robert and his team were wrestled against the wall and clubbed by their attackers.

Ambushed and outnumbered, they were not going to win this battle. Their only hope was to escape.

CHAPTER 25

It had taken only a phone call for Amanda to arrange an appointment with the daytime manager at the *Torrevecchia*. He was eager to show off the older areas of the hotel and describe the changes that had been made.

"That was easy," Amanda said as she hung up her cell phone and grinned at Julia. "Why don't you meet with him? There's no need for both of us to go. I'll see what I can find out about the other tower remnants in the area."

Julia's appointment was during the afternoon siesta, when business in the hotel would be slow. She called Nic after breakfast. He was busy with a couple of new cases and apologized for not spending more time with her the past couple of days. "I miss you, *cara*," he whispered into the phone. "Let's go out to dinner tomorrow."

"I miss you too, Nic," she said. "Dinner would be lovely."

She spent the rest of the morning strolling through the streets near the center of the city, looking for evidence of other tower connections she and Amanda might want to investigate. By the time she arrived at the *Torrevecchia*, the manager was waiting for her at the front desk.

"I'm so delighted you are interested in the history of this place," he said. "Most American tourists don't seem to care about its past—which was really quite fascinating and important. Maybe you can change that."

"I think it will provide an interesting sidelight to the article I am writing," she answered. Amanda had suggested to her that she should use that as an explanation for her curiosity about buildings in the historic center, adding, "Whatever you find out might very well be the basis for another article you can pitch to your editor back home." Julia liked that idea. Another article would give her a reason for spending more time in Florence—with Nic.

The hotel manager, who insisted she call him Matteo, proudly showed her all the areas on the ground floor, pointing out the changes that had come in the oldest part of the building when the renovation was done. Their last stop was in the hotel bar. "The most difficult part of the remodel was here. We gutted the whole area and turned what remained of the tower into a fireplace."

"So there's nothing left of the tower structure?"

"It was gone a long time ago, I'm told. It had fallen into disuse."

"I've been in this bar," Julia insisted. "And I've heard some unusual sounds coming from that part of the room. What causes that?"

Matteo looked surprised and paused before he answered. "Even though the renovation was recent, there could still be some cracks in the fireplace that allow the wind to enter. Or contractions when the fire is lit. Maybe street noise from the piazza outside. But I can assure you, it is very solid and very secure."

Julia had one last point to press. "Could the sounds be coming from the basement, up into the tower?"

Matteo shook his head. "You don't understand. There's nothing below this level now. Any basement, if it ever existed, was filled in long ago." He smiled and lowered his voice. "You're not alone in thinking you hear sounds coming from that end of the bar. Other guests have mentioned that too. Trust me. It's just a fireplace."

Impressed by the man's knowledge of the building's history and convinced of his sincerity, Julia thanked him for the tour. "This is such a lovely hotel, and its history is enchanting. I'll make sure to mention it in my article."

Matteo beamed as he grabbed her hand and kissed it. "Thank you, *signorina*. And please come back to visit us again. You are always welcome here."

On her way through the piazza, heading back to her *pensione*, she couldn't help but feel disappointed. She had been so certain that the hotel held hidden places and maybe even some clues to Robert's whereabouts. *I hope Amanda has had better luck.*

Eager to compare notes, Julia arrived early for dinner and watched for her friend to arrive. Amanda didn't come, which seemed odd. She had told Julia once that she preferred to eat at the hotel, rather than—as she put it—spend an outrageous amount of money at a local restaurant.

After lingering at her table when her dinner was over, Julia stopped by Amanda's room. She tapped on the door. No response. She tried again, pounding harder. Still no response.

"Amanda, are you in there?" she called. When no

answer came, she stepped away from the door and raised a trembling hand to her lips. *My God. Did I get her into some kind of trouble?*

She retreated to her room to decide what to do. If Amanda was in danger, she couldn't very well ignore that. *I have to try to find her—help her if necessary.* But should she do it by herself? Asking Nic was out of the question. He had made it clear he was busy with other cases, and he would also be upset with her for her amateurish investigation gone awry.

From her conversation with Amanda over breakfast, she knew the woman's destination for the day—one of the neighborhoods with still-visible remnants of an old tower structure.

That's not too far from here. And it's still early enough in the evening that businesses will be open, and people will be around. The chance that she would be attacked as she had been the night before seemed remote, so she decided to retrace the steps she assumed Amanda had taken.

The center of the city was crowded with tourists. She felt safer, but it was harder to catch glimpses of her friend amid so many people. She found herself studying every group passing her in the piazzas and on the sidewalks. As she approached the first street Amanda had gone to investigate, she stopped, alarmed by what she saw.

It was her worst fear. An ambulance was parked in front of a row of shops, lights flashing. A small crowd of onlookers watched as the emergency crew lifted a stretcher where a victim lay covered with a blanket, a tuft of gray hair sticking out from beneath the covers. Alongside the ambulance, watching the crew as it tended to the victim, was Nic.

The ambulance finally moved slowly down the narrow

passage, siren blaring, on its way to a hospital. As it did, Nic turned to those standing nearby. Notebook in hand, he began to interview witnesses, just as he had after Piero Manca's collapse in the piazza outside the *Hotel Torrevecchia*. Julia watched, backed against the sturdy stone wall of a building bordering the street. When Nic finished his interviews, he closed his notebook, looked around, and saw her. He walked toward her and, as he came close, reached for her hand. "What are you doing here?" he asked.

"I think the person the ambulance just took away may be a friend of mine from the *pensione*. When she didn't come to dinner, I was worried. That wasn't like her. So I came looking for her."

Nic stepped back and scowled at her. "Why did you choose this neighborhood?"

"Because she and I talked over breakfast this morning, and she told me she would be here today to check out the towers."

"Check out the towers? Why? What are you looking for?" Julia could tell he was annoyed. Should she tell him about the investigation she and Amanda had planned? She knew that might anger him even more. But maybe he would be willing to help now that someone had been injured.

"We talked last night. I told her about Robert's disappearance and how I wanted to find him. She thought maybe if he was being held somewhere, it might be in one of the tower neighborhoods. She knows the city well."

"You went ahead and started looking for him on your own after I told you not to get involved?" he asked, his voice rising. "After I warned you there was a risk of your getting injured?"

"I was injured anyway. Someone attacked me on the way home last night. Amanda was concerned about me. That's why she offered to help."

"You were attacked? How? Why didn't you tell me?"

"Because you made it clear you didn't want to be bothered," she said. Now she was angry too. "If you hadn't refused to help me look for Robert, or if you had at least told me enough about the police awareness of his disappearance to let me know if he was in danger, this wouldn't have happened to Amanda."

"Come on! The person they just took away is a guy who was hurt in a bar fight. This has nothing to do with Amanda. And what you're saying about Robert makes no sense."

"You told me that the police were aware of Robert's disappearance, but you wouldn't tell me if they were doing anything to find him. And you made it clear that you weren't willing to help me look for him."

"I was doing that to protect you, Julia," Nic began and reached out to her again.

"I don't need that, Nic," she said, brushing him away. "Your kind of protection is endangering someone I care about."

She turned and hurried down the street, leaving Nic staring after her. Once in the piazza, she fell into the bustling crowd of tourists enjoying the city's nightlife and headed toward the *Pensione Europa*, struggling with the emotions of her argument with Nic. When she approached her hotel, she didn't notice the figure huddled in the darkness near the entrance.

"Julia?" The question was barely audible.

She swirled and saw a man stagger out of the shadows.

His mouth and jaw were bruised and one of his eyes was swollen shut. But she recognized him.

"Robert!"

He reached out to her, slumping into her arms. Touching a finger to her lips, he whispered, "Shhh. I shouldn't be here."

She hugged him tight and steadied him. "What's happened to you? Where have you been?" she asked.

"I've been busy." He raised his head and looked around. "But this isn't the place to talk. Can we go to your room?"

CHAPTER 26

On their way upstairs, both were silent. Robert leaned against the back wall of the elevator, and Julia put her arm around his waist. When they arrived at her floor, she held him up as they struggled down the hall. She opened the door to her room, and he followed her inside, stumbling a bit before he threw himself onto the loveseat. He lay back and closed his eyes.

Flipping the switch that turned on the ceiling light, Julia could see Robert was exhausted as well as battered. Eager as she was to find out where he had been and what he had been up to, she knew she had to let him rest, so she busied herself with clearing out the clutter she had left behind earlier in the evening. She had long since moved the coffee pot, cups, and glasses from the side table to the top of the refrigerator and replaced them with her laptop and notebooks. Now, she added to them the stack of guidebooks she had been reading before she headed for her appointment at *Hotel Torrevecchia*. With those materials neatly in place, she hung her jacket and scarf in the wardrobe and looped the strap of her purse over one of the bed posts.

Robert had fallen asleep. She closed the window shutters, turned down the ceiling light in the room, and poured a glass of *Pinot Grigio* from a bottle she had stashed in the refrigerator. With everything more in order, she settled onto the chair next to the couch and waited for him to wake up.

After a while, Robert's eyes fluttered open. He looked at Julia and smiled.

"Thanks. It feels good to be somewhere warm and cozy for a change."

"How long were you waiting outside?" she asked.

"I hadn't been there long. I was trying to decide if I should go into the hotel and ask for you at the desk. I was just lucky you came by when you did."

He turned his head and sized up the room. "This place looks the same as it did when I stayed here. Are you enjoying it?"

"This isn't exactly the kind of hotel that ever changes, but I like it. It took some getting used to. The staff is very friendly. And the other guests have become almost like family to me."

She paused, hoping silence would prompt him to say more. Running his hand through his hair, he cleared his throat. "I know I owe you an explanation." He looked at her, waiting for a response. She said nothing.

"I've been following some leads I found about the stuff going on in the neighborhood near where you were staying. I hooked up with some other people who were also concerned about the situation there. We've been working together, investigating."

"Investigating?"

"Just following leads. Looking into things that don't seem legit."

"Isn't that what the police are supposed to do? Why is it up to you and your...friends?"

"Because the police have enough to do with crimes that have clearly been committed. My friends and I are trying to expose...hidden crimes, I guess you could call them. Once we have enough information about them, we can report them to the police."

Julia got up and walked over to the window and stared back at Robert. She took another sip of wine. "You know how crazy that sounds?" she asked.

Robert sat up and fingered his bruised lip before answering. "It may sound crazy, but it's important that we do it. There's a lot of underground criminal activity here, the same as in other big cities. Not the kind of thing police bother with until the extent of it is revealed."

"Is it worth it? Ending up like you are now? What happened?"

"A few of us have been tracking comings and goings at a place close to your old hotel. We're pretty sure there may be something illegal going on there. We think women are in danger."

"Women in danger?" Julia asked. "In what way?"

Robert was clearly uncomfortable sharing details with her. He didn't want to alarm her. "Sex trafficking. It's very entrenched in some parts of the city, operating out of sight, beyond what the police can control—or what they choose to control."

Julia walked over to the loveseat and sat down next to Robert. "What are you talking about? Prostitution?"

"Prostitution is legal in Italy, if you mean streetwalkers. This is sex slavery. Young women who come here from other parts of Italy or other countries are lured into prostitution and basically held captive, and forced to perform sexual acts. They can't escape because they don't get to keep most of the money paid for their services. And they have no place else to go."

Julia closed her eyes and covered her mouth with her hand. What he was describing was making her stomach turn. "That's awful," she said. "Is it just here in Italy?"

"No, it's found in countries all over the world. Even in the States."

It was clear that Robert's investigations had taken him into a very unsavory and dangerous part of life in Florence. *Am I in jeopardy, too?* She needed to know more.

"How did you get hurt?"

Robert shook his head. "I'm not sure," he answered. "We had planned to enter a building and check it out to see if we found any women held captive there. Maybe even help them escape. We were told there hadn't been any men entering the place for several hours, so it seemed safe to us. But we were wrong. As soon as we got inside, we were grabbed and beaten. One of us was badly hurt. I was lucky to find a back door where I escaped. I couldn't think of any place I could go right at that moment. That's why I came here."

"What happened to the others who were with you?"

"I don't know. I hope they got away."

Neither said anything for several minutes. Finally, Julia leaned over and took a closer look at Robert's face. "You really should go to an emergency room for your injuries."

"I can't. Those goons will be looking for me to go to a hospital. Don't you see? If they know where I am, they'll come after me. I know too much about them now."

He saw the alarm in Julia's eyes. "Look," he added.

"I'll have to keep out of sight until I can figure out what to do next...and where to go." Julia started to object, but Robert grabbed her hand and held it tight. "You're safe," he said softly. "They don't know who you are or that you have any connection with me, so they won't have any idea that I've come here. Let me stay with you tonight. Please."

Julia rubbed her forehead, trying to sort out her feelings, trying to make sense of what Robert had told her. Finally, she sighed. "Then let me at least fix an ice pack for you. Those bruises are going to get worse if we don't do something about them."

She insisted that Robert share the bed with her, but they didn't sleep. He was in too much pain because of his injuries, and she was too worried, both about him and about Amanda. They lay awake for much of the night talking. She told him about all she had done to try to find out what had happened to him. Amanda's help was crucial, and her failure to come back to the hotel that night worried her. Robert was surprised to hear that Amanda had been involved. He knew her—or knew of her. "She's a tour guide, isn't she? Tweed suits and sensible shoes? She's been in the business for years."

"Do you think she might be in danger?"

"I'm not sure. She knows her way around this city. And she's familiar with its people. I think she'd have a good idea of who and what to avoid."

By dawn, both were so exhausted they had dozed off. Julia was awakened by streaks of daylight filtering through the shutters. She got out of bed quietly and freshened up enough to head to breakfast, leaving Robert still sleeping. In the dining room, she lingered after she had finished her meal, hoping to see Amanda, but her friend didn't come.

What should I do next? She would do all she could for Robert, of course. And maybe he could help her find out what, if anything, had happened to Amanda. She couldn't help feeling that the other woman's welfare was very much linked to her own.

For now, she would have to make sure Robert was getting food while he stayed in hiding in her room. Scooping several breakfast pastries into her napkin, she poured a cup of espresso for him and walked out of the dining room. Upstairs, juggling everything in one hand, she unlocked the door to her room with the other.

Robert wasn't on the bed anymore, so she kicked the door shut and put his breakfast on the coffee table. "Robert?" she called, thinking he was in the bathroom. She walked over to that side of the room and called again. "Robert?"

No answer. She opened the bathroom door and peeked inside. He wasn't there. It wasn't until she hurried back over to the bed that she found the note he had left on the pillow and read its brief, scrawled message.

"Dearest Julia. Once again, I haven't leveled with you entirely. I know Amanda better than I let on last night. I don't know where she is now, and I can't tell you where I am going to be for a while because I don't want to get you caught up in what's going on. Just know this. I'm pretty sure Amanda is safe. She has lots of friends she can turn to for help or shelter. I will reach out to you again to let you know more when I'm sure I'm not putting you at risk. Thank you for last night. Love, R."

Winds gusted outside the hotel. Was it the kind of weather that would make it hard for Robert to find a comfortable place where he could recuperate? Striding over to the window, she threw open the inside and outside shutters. Scattered groups of people were hurrying along the sidewalk, wrapped in heavy coats and holding onto their hats. Sunbeams sparkled on the Arno rippling below. It was going to be another blustery but beautiful spring day.

She studied Robert's note again and folded it up: *At least I know what he has been up to. And he is safe—for the time being. So is Amanda—maybe—hidden someplace for a while. Apparently, I'm on my own again.*

She closed the shutters and walked over to her makeshift desk, tucking the folded paper inside one of the guidebooks stacked there. Until she knew who Robert was convinced would come looking for him, no other eyes should see it. *I have to protect his secrets. But will he show up again?*

CHAPTER 27

The cluttered space was dark and musty. Rancid smells and mold in the ancient basement set off Amanda's allergies, but, sneezing every few paces, she kept inching along the uneven floor, out of the underground chamber and into a cramped passageway that led toward what appeared to be a barrier of some sort at the end. Dressed in a borrowed sweatsuit and her trusty tennis shoes, she was prepared for the conditions.

She stopped and looked back at her companion. Renzo was several feet behind her, and his breathing was labored. *It was probably not a good idea to have asked him to join her on this mission.* His bulk and physical condition made it hard for him to keep up with her, and he was clearly uncomfortable in the narrow space they had entered. But he had insisted on coming with her.

The substructure she had asked to see in the old tower building lay beneath the leather crafts store he and his family had owned for generations. If she wanted to explore its secrets, he told her, he wanted to be with her, to help her uncover any mysteries it concealed. And besides, he and Amanda had known each other for years. More than friends at one time. He couldn't let her risk injury while exploring the long-neglected area by herself. It would violate every protective instinct he had for her, every caring feeling they had once shared.

He struggled to catch up to her. She paused and motioned for him to stay still. "Listen!" she whispered. "What was that?"

He strained and couldn't hear anything for a moment. And then...there it was. A sound. A cry coming from somewhere further down the passageway. He crept closer to Amanda, who was standing still, hand cupped to her ear, "That's a girl's voice, isn't it?" he whispered.

She nodded. "I think so."

"But how can anyone be down here without me knowing about it? They would have to go through our building."

"There must be another way in. But that's not the most important question right now. Is someone hurt? It sounds like she's crying."

Amanda forged ahead, moving as quickly as she could, wriggling through the narrow space. Renzo followed, bracing his arms against the rugged walls.

Clearing away the debris that concealed a wooden door at the end of the passageway, Amanda pushed the barrier open and stepped into a dungeon-like room, unfinished except for a shelf carved out of the stone on one side. A shaft of light entering through a barred window near the ceiling cast a beam on two figures huddled close together on the ledge. Scantily clothed, two young girls clung to each other. One of them, dark-haired and buxom, appeared to be slightly older. Amanda guessed she was about 17 or 18 years old. The other was younger and smaller. Blonde, frail, and shaking, she was crying.

Amanda approached them slowly. *I have to be careful. They're already frightened.* The dark-haired girl saw her and clutched her companion even tighter.

"Don't be afraid," Amanda said, keeping her voice soft and reassuring. "We are here to help." She could see that their trembling wasn't just from fear. They were also very cold. "Would you like a blanket or something to keep you warm?"

The two girls looked at her without comprehending. *They don't speak English,* Amanda realized. She tried again in Italian. This time, the dark-haired girl nodded. Her companion stopped crying and looked directly at Amanda as she wiped the tears from her eyes. But when Renzo crawled into the room and approached, the two hugged each other again and the blonde buried her head in her companion's shoulder.

"Renzo, there's something about you that frightens them. Back off. Let me talk to them by myself."

Renzo hesitated. He didn't want to leave Amanda in this strange and threatening place, but she was right. For some reason, his presence was upsetting to the girls. If he left, he could try to do something that would make the situation better. "There are some blankets in the storage area under my shop," he offered. "I'll bring a couple of them here."

Amanda nodded her approval. "Tell me how you got here," Renzo heard her say as he left the room and headed back down the passageway.

When he came back, carrying a pair of blankets and castaway coats, he stood quietly just inside the entry to the room, waiting for a sign that the girls were comfortable with his presence. Amanda was sitting on the stone ledge next to the two girls. The blonde was speaking in a voice that was so timid it was almost inaudible. Her words came in bursts, a few at a time. She was struggling to be understood. It was clear that Italian wasn't her native language. She paused and wiped her nose with the back of her hand.

"That's when we ran away," she said to Amanda. "They weren't looking."

"We thought this was a way out, but we were wrong," the dark-haired girl added. "We can't go back now. They'll beat us again. Probably worse than ever."

Renzo cleared his throat, announcing his return, and held out the coats and blankets. The girls leaped off the ledge and grabbed the coats from him. As they slipped their arms through the sleeves and pulled the coarse fabric around them, they even managed a shy smile at Renzo. It didn't matter that the coats were old and several sizes too large, they provided the warmth the youngsters needed. As they sat back down on the ledge, they took the blankets that Renzo had brought and wrapped them tight around their legs, snuggling close together.

"They have been through a horrifying experience," Amanda said to Renzo, speaking in English to keep the girls from hearing the alarm she felt about their story. "They came here to find work so they could send money back to their homes up north. Their families are very poor. But they were kidnapped and sold into sex slavery by the men who had promised them jobs."

"Sex slavery? Where?"

"Here in Florence. Somewhere in this neighborhood. They and several women are kept in a place where they are forced to have sex with several men a day. They don't get to keep the money, so they would have no way of providing for themselves even if they managed to escape."

"But the dark-haired girl just said they did get out," Renzo said. "Isn't that how they ended up here?"

Amanda paused before she answered. "They got out when there was some sort of raid on their quarters. Apparently, an attempted rescue of the women held captive there. It failed, but there was enough confusion that these two escaped into a cellar under their building. They followed crawl spaces that led them here, trapped."

Amanda stopped and looked down at the blonde who was resting against her shoulder. "I'm afraid they will be badly hurt if they go back. We have to help them."

"Help them? How?"

"I'm not sure. But we need to get them out of here. Back to your store where maybe we can give them a better place to rest until we figure out what to do next."

CHAPTER 28

The doctor sat in a high-backed leather chair, sipping a glass of *vin santo,* as he did every evening after dinner. The warmth of the fireplace in his library was particularly welcome on this chilly evening. He watched its flames flicker and flutter, caught in downdrafts from the gusts outside. It was good to be safe at home. This was not a night to be out. Not just because of the weather. There were always other reasons to be wary.

A rap at the window—in the rhythmic code of the group—startled him. Throwing off the blanket that he had draped across his legs, he rose and walked out of the library to the front door and unlocked it, opening it wide.

"What took you so long?" a voice demanded. "It's cold out here."

Three men entered, their faces half covered by the hoods on their coats. One was injured, maybe seriously, as best as could be told from the way the other two half-carried him over the threshold. The doctor put his arm around the man's waist, helping him farther into the entryway. "Let's get him to a place where he's more comfortable," he said. "I want to see how badly hurt he is."

The man was large and heavy. His two companions struggled to move him into a room tucked behind the winding staircase that led down from the upper floor of the house and laid him on a daybed positioned against the back wall. The doctor sat down next to him where he could examine his wounds more closely, studying the bruises on his face, pointing a flashlight in his eyes, and gently rotating his arms and shoulders. After a few minutes, the doctor leaned back and looked at the other two.

"I don't think he's too bad," he said. "There are several contusions on his face and his arms, but there don't seem to be any broken bones. He may have a concussion, however, so it would be best if he stayed here for a day or two."

"Won't somebody notice that he is here?" the tallest of the men asked. "And be curious about who he is and how he got hurt?"

"When our children were young, this is where their nanny stayed. But that was a long time ago. We never use this room anymore, except for occasional houseguests. And my wife has gone to spend the week with our son and his family in Milano. She won't be back for several days. No one will see him except me. He can go back to his own home as soon as he feels better. I see no need for him to go to a hospital."

The tall man heaved a sigh of relief. "Can we stay here too? It'll be safer for us to go to our own homes in daylight. And we need to think through with each other—and with you—what went wrong and what should be our next steps."

"OK. But just for one night. You'll have to sleep in the library. I'll talk to you there after I finish here."

When he was confident that he had done all that was needed to dress the injured man's wounds, the doctor returned to his library, where the other two sat opposite each other on couches in the middle of the room. They watched as he approached them, their faces reflecting concern for their friend.

"He'll be all right," he assured them and slumped into the easy chair next to them. "I wasn't expecting you," he said. "Why did you risk coming here? What went wrong?" It had always been understood that he wouldn't be brought into the work of the group unless the situation was dire.

"An ambush," the tall man answered. The doctor knew him only as Sandro. "We thought the women in the building were alone, but they weren't. As soon as we went upstairs to find them, we were attacked by several men who were hiding in one of the rooms. "Giuseppe," he said, pointing in the direction of their injured companion, "held them off until we could get out. If he hadn't, none of us would have been spared. We managed to fight back enough that we could all escape."

"There were only three of you?"

"There was a fourth, besides Antonio and Giuseppe and me. He took quite a beating too. But he headed in another direction when we ran away. I don't know what happened to him. Look, we know we risk exposing you by coming here, but you're the only one who can provide medical help. We can't go to a hospital without revealing who we are and what we were doing. That would get the police involved. And we're not ready for that."

. . .

Robert staggered along the street leading to the building he hoped would be a safe haven. He tapped loudly on the front door, using the secret code.

The sound woke up everyone inside. It was morning, and no one had slept well. As Sandro and Antonio listened, the doctor returned to the library, followed by Robert, disheveled and limping into the room.

So the others made it here safely. Robert sighed with relief. He wasn't surprised to see them at the doctor's house. It was one of their agreed-upon places to rendezvous but to be used only as a last resort. It was the obvious place to gather if any team members were badly injured.

The doctor checked him out carefully. The bruises on his face were painful but not serious. No concussion or broken bones, he was assured. The ice pack Julia had given him had kept the swelling down, and he was already feeling better.

The doctor left the library for a few moments to check on Giuseppe in the guest room behind the staircase and to prepare breakfast for the rest of the group. Sandro and Antonio compared notes with Robert on what had gone wrong with their rescue mission. "Somebody must have tipped them off," Sandro said. "They were obviously ready for us."

"But who?" Robert asked. "Members of our group were the only ones who knew where we were going."

"Maybe, "Sandro answered, clenching his teeth. "Who else could it be? Somebody betrayed us. And I'm thinking the same thing may have happened to the two of us who were attacked in front of the Duomo. Somebody knew who they were and where they would be most vulnerable to attack."

The three were silent as they realized the consequences

for their group. They had all taken a vow to protect each other at all costs and never to reveal the details of the mission they had sworn to support. Trust was crucial to their work. Robert was stunned. *If Sandro's suspicions are valid...everyone is in danger.*

When the doctor returned with a tray of pastries and fruit, they shared their concerns with him. As they ate, they tried to sort out what they should do next.

CHAPTER 29

It was an impulse at first, born out of the boredom she felt at being stuck in her hotel, waiting to hear from others. Curled up and resting on the loveseat in her room, Julia passed the time by browsing through the guidebooks that had earlier provided useful information about tower neighborhoods. And then she decided to go over the proofs of the photos she had taken for her article on travel in the millennium, an idle diversion at first. Examining them critically, studying the backgrounds, she was able to see past the details that had first had her interest. Figures captured without their knowledge. A grainy panorama of ordinary, uneventful Florentine life.

Or was it? A pattern began to emerge, not in all shots, but in a few scenes near the tower neighborhoods. Young girls huddled in doorways, watching passersby. In one photo, they were being confronted by a well-dressed older man. Then, in the next shots in the series, all of them were missing, replaced by a younger man striding along the street, looking at something out of the frame ahead of him. A final image, in the deep background, blurred but still recognizable, was the mysterious person who had attacked her in the passageway near the hotel. He wasn't wearing the black T-shirt and slacks by which she had come to recognize him, but his face was unmistakable. Scowling, eyes riveted on the action unfolding in front of him.

Why didn't I notice him when I was photographing the scenes? Maybe it was because of the growing numbers of tourists flooding the downtown sites. He didn't stand out in the crowds. *But what was he doing there?* He seemed to be looking at something, but what exactly?

She put the proofs on the coffee table and sat up, her heart pounding. She didn't remember seeing him in her recent excursions in the city. The one exception—her late-night encounter in the street near her hotel—had caught her by surprise. Had he been near her more often, watching her, following her? She had grown so comfortable in her surroundings that it had never occurred to her that there might be an ongoing element of danger lurking there.

The thought was chilling. *Who was he?* She had to find out, but who could help? After last night's argument with Nic, she probably wouldn't hear from him for a while. Amanda and Robert—they might know what to do, but where were they? Was Amanda somewhere safe?

Carlo. Of course! She needed to call him anyway. He wouldn't be in touch unless he had something new to report, but he would no doubt be relieved to hear about Robert. And if she told him about the man in the T-shirt and showed him the photo—who knows? Maybe Carlo would recognize him or have some idea of who he might be.

It was worth a try. She called his office and found him

in. They arranged to meet for coffee and a snack that afternoon.

That left most of the morning and the lunch hour for her to explore the neighborhood where she had inadvertently captured on film the mysterious encounter between the young girls and the older man.

Slipping into walking shoes and a jacket, she gathered up her camera bag, headed out her door toward the elevator—and ran into Amanda, shuffling down the hallway toward her room, much more casually dressed than usual, in sweats and tennis shoes that were covered with dirt and debris.

"Where have you been? Are you okay?" Julia exclaimed. "I've been worried sick about you."

Amanda paused and leaned against the wall. "I'm fine. But I'm exhausted. You won't believe the night I've had. Give me a few hours to catch up on my sleep, and I'll tell you all about it over dinner."

"That's a deal," Julia said, smiling. "Here, let me help you to your room."

On another day, Amanda probably would have resisted Julia's offer, but this time, she linked arms with her younger friend and let her lead the way. "You'd think I would learn that I'm too old to be getting involved in things that are beyond my control, wouldn't you?" she chuckled as they moved slowly down the hall.

When they arrived at her room, Amanda unlocked the door and patted Julia's arm. "Thank you," she said with a sleepy smile. "I promise I'll be alright. You go and enjoy whatever you were planning to do when you ran into me."

Julia reached out impulsively and hugged her. "I'm so glad you're safe," she whispered. "I'll look for you at dinner."

She walked back down the hallway and took the elevator to the reception area. The desk clerk saw her as she headed toward the stairs and waved to get her attention. *"Signorina!* I was about to go to your room. Someone has sent you a gift."

Julia approached the desk where a huge vase sat, filled with a fragrant mix of wildflowers. A note lay nestled within the bouquet of pink, red and purple blossoms. It was from Nic.

"Cara. I'm so sorry I upset you last night. I promise I'll make it up to you. Dinner tomorrow? I'll meet you at our usual time. I love you. Nic"

She carried the vase back to her room, juggling it in one arm as she opened the door. Once inside, she arranged it on the coffee table, sat down on the loveseat, and studied the bouquet, her hand tucked under her chin. "As if things weren't complicated enough today, he has to do this," she murmured, reaching out and touching the petals gently. "Is this his way of reclaiming control of our relationship?" It was the kind of thing Bill would do after an argument. *But Nic isn't like Bill. Or is he?*

After reading Nic's note one more time, she sighed, tucked it back inside the flowers, and left her room again, headed to the tower neighborhoods she had photographed, prepared to explore them once again with an eye for activities she hadn't noticed before.

Because he hadn't had time for lunch, Carlo had suggested meeting at a small bakery and sandwich stop in the historic core of the city. As Julia expected, he was relieved to hear that Robert had come to see her, but he was alarmed by her account of the raid on the sex trafficking den.

"That was incredibly foolish. Robert and his companions may be sincere in their concern about sex slavery, but they won't put a stop to it with such harebrained escapades."

"So sex trafficking really is a problem here?"

"Of course it is," he said, taking a huge bite out of the lampredotto and pecorino panino he had ordered, using a napkin to wipe the sauce dripping down his chin. "It's a problem throughout the world. Italy isn't the only country where it's found."

"So why is it dangerous to try to expose it and free the victims? That's all Robert and his friends were trying to do."

Carlo waved away her comment. "It's dangerous because those running the trafficking operations—especially if they are Mafia connected—are merciless. They won't be stopped by amateurs who don't know what they are doing." Exasperated, he put the sandwich back on its plate and leaned back in his chair.

"I have a colleague who is writing a book about the problem," he said. "He approaches it very carefully—using intermediaries, being careful in his research. Not letting the traffickers know who he is or what he is up to. It's the only safe way to learn about it. When he has enough information, he'll turn it over to the police. And eventually publish the results of his research, of course."

He was clearly bothered, and Julia didn't want to upset him any further. Changing the subject, she described her encounters with the man in the black T-shirt and showed Carlo the photograph with the man lingering in the background. "He seems to spend a lot of time in the area near my old hotel. Have you ever seen him around?"

Carlo took the photograph and studied it closely. He was silent as he handed it back to her. "I think I've seen him before," he said finally. "But I can't tell you who he is." He shrugged his shoulders. "I'm sorry. I wish I could be more helpful."

Julia was shocked. "You aren't going to tell me if I'm in danger?"

Carlo took a while to respond. Almost too long. He seemed to be considering how much to share with Julia. He picked up the sandwich on his plate and picked at the crust. Finally, he spoke. "I didn't say you're in danger. Frankly, I don't know if you are. But if you feel threatened, you should avoid him if you can."

Julia swallowed. "That's not exactly reassuring. Don't you understand? I don't seek him out—he just seems to be following me. So simply telling me to avoid him isn't very helpful," she added, loudly enough to make other customers in the bar turn and look at her.

Lowering his voice to calm her, Carlo answered, "I really can't say anything more. If I thought he was a threat to you, believe me, I'd let you know."

He continued to concentrate on his sandwich, deliberately avoiding Julia's gaze. *This is so unlike Carlo. Should I just get up and leave?*

The silence between them grew until Carlo looked at her and reached across the table to touch her hand.

"There may be something I can do for you," he said. "I can help you on the other matter you're curious about. I'll get you some information about sex trafficking in Italy if you're truly interested in finding out more about it."

Julia was intrigued by the offer. Her anger subsided a

bit. "Can you get me an appointment with your colleague? The one who is studying sex trafficking?"

Her question seemed to catch Carlo by surprise. He shrugged and took another bite out of his sandwich and washed it down with a swallow of carbonated water. "I'll ask him if he's willing to talk to you," he said. "That's all I can promise."

CHAPTER 30

Amanda was quieter than usual at dinner. Settling into her place at the table opposite Julia, she motioned to the waiter, who brought with him a glass of the Chianti she ordered every night, a request so predictable he didn't even have to ask. "I'll have the usual" was all she needed to say. Her dinner choices were slightly more varied, but they always started with pasta, followed by an entree. Often, the meat would be veal. A salad would round out her dining.

Julia couldn't help but smile at her friend's commitment to her routine. Amanda noticed. "First things first," she smiled as she raised her glass of Chianti in Julia's direction. *"Cin cin."*

"You still look tired," Julia said, touching her own glass of *pinot grigio* to Amanda's. They watched as the waiter arrived with their first courses.

"I am," Amanda answered. "Last night was brutal, in more ways than one." Talking as she enjoyed a pasta course of tagliolini and truffles, she launched into a description of her long night exploring the passageway leading from the building where her friend Renzo and his family had long owned their leather crafts business. The two of them had started out in the basement beneath his shop, she said. It was there that they found a tunnel that wound, as best they could tell, beneath several other structures. "I've known Renzo for a long time, and I remembered that he had told me that his shop was in a building that had once been part of a tower complex. That's why I started there. I felt safe having him along with me. And I knew I could borrow some clothes from him that would be better suited to poking around in filthy cellars."

She finished eating her pasta and looked at Julia with tears in her eyes. "The worst of it was the horrifying story we heard from the two girls we found in the secret room at the end of the tunnel. I couldn't stop thinking about it after I came back here this morning. I had trouble getting to sleep, it bothered me so much."

"What was their story?"

"About being sex slaves. Forced by sex traffickers to sell themselves. I can't believe such a cruel crime continues to go on in what I've always thought were more enlightened times. I mean, this is even more harmful to women than some of the stuff that happened here centuries ago."

"You mean the time of the women's prison?" The two of them had earlier shared their fascination with its history in the old tower.

"Yes. Worse even. The women's prison just kept women in their place. The sex trade exploits and abuses them."

Julia was struggling to understand why her friend had persisted in a situation that so obviously disturbed her. "Amanda, what made you keep going last night? Why were you so sure there was something at the end of the passageway?"

"Curiosity, maybe. Or a hunch that there had to be something linking those old buildings. Something left over from so long ago that nobody would think to look there. Honestly, I don't know. I just somehow felt I had to stay with it. And as we approached the end of the tunnel, we heard someone crying. At that point, of course, we couldn't stop. We found the door behind a bunch of junk—actually, less a door than a boarded-up hole. Renzo and I cleared away the rubble, and when I opened the passageway...I saw the two girls. I talked to them for quite a while. Enough to gain their trust, so they felt comfortable telling me about what had happened to them."

"Did they live in the room where you found them?"

"Oh no. It was just luck that Renzo and I were exploring the passage that led into that place. They had escaped from the building where they had been held captive. Where we found them wasn't livable space at all. Very cold, and they weren't wearing much clothing. I don't know what would have become of them if we hadn't found them."

When Amanda described the way the girls had been able to slip away from their captors because of a failed rescue attempt, Julia stopped eating and stared at her. "That sounds like it may have been Robert and his team."

"Robert? Why would he have been there?"

"Amanda, I was going to tell you about Robert staying here last night. He had just come from a fight at a sex trafficking operation that sounds very much like the one you heard about from the two girls."

Julia's account of Robert's unsuccessful attempt at rescuing women held as sex slaves stunned Amanda. She listened attentively, not wanting to interrupt, nodding occasionally at details that seemed to coincide with what the girls had told her. When Julia finished, she took a long sip of Chianti, and shook her head. "Julia," she said, "it may very well have been the same raid. Two of them taking place at the same time seems unlikely."

The two women were quiet for a moment. "Where is Robert now?" Amanda asked.

"I don't know. He was gone by the time I got back from breakfast. He left a note. I think he went someplace safe where he could be treated for his injuries. He didn't tell me where."

"I wish he had told you. And I'm curious about that mysterious group he's part of, if it's as intent as it seems to be in trying to put an end to sex trafficking."

"If it's the only one, wouldn't it stand out?" Julia asked.

"Actually, it isn't. That's what Renzo and I found out this morning. There are other groups or organizations, but they help the victims. Renzo's priest told him about a shelter for women who escaped or were rescued. That's where we took the girls: A safe house where they will be given food and other assistance. Where they can recover."

"I'd like to hear about the shelter," Julia said. This was new information to her, and she was eager to learn. "Would Renzo be willing to talk to me—to us?"

"We can ask. He told me the girls who are housed there are protected because the traffickers might retaliate against them or their relatives. As long as we don't tell anyone else...." She looked hard at Julia and added, "or write anything about it."

Julia nodded. "I won't do anything that will disclose their identity or where they are staying. I promise."

CHAPTER 31

The next morning, Carlo called the *pensione*. Julia had just finished breakfast in the dining room and was looking forward to a more relaxing day on her own, but his tone was urgent. "I told my colleague—the one who is doing research on sex trafficking—about Robert and the raid where he and his friends were attacked. He wants to meet with you to find out what else you know."

"I'll meet him anywhere and anytime he wants," she said, excited at the prospect of talking to someone who might be able to help Robert.

"Let's meet for lunch. My department is in an area away from the center of the city, so my colleague and I will be at a sandwich shop near a branch of the university closer to your *pensione*. I'll introduce you to him."

"Thank you, Carlo! I'll see you there."

"Oh, by the way. Bring your photos of the man you suspect has been following you. My colleague might be able to help you with that, too."

Hopeful about the prospect of getting positive news

about Robert, she grabbed her camera bag, stuffed the photo proofs inside, and headed toward the elevator. She stopped to tap on Amanda's door, to let her know where she was going, but there was no answer. "Probably sightseeing," she thought. Amanda had talked to her at breakfast and mentioned that she was going to check in with Renzo and then visit the Accademia.

"My holiday will end soon," she explained to Julia. "I have a few favorite places I absolutely must see again before I leave."

For the rest of the morning, Julia was also ready for her own sightseeing. The Museo San Marco, with its frescoes by Fra Angelico, was close to the place Carlo had recommended, so she decided to spend the morning there before joining the two men for lunch. The piazza surrounding the convent where the museum was located was busy with students and tourists. There was a vibrancy to the scene that reminded her of what she loved about Florence.

She arrived at the sandwich shop just before noon. Carlo was already there, early as usual. The man sitting with him at an outside table was so unlike him in appearance and demeanor Julia couldn't help but smile. They both stood as she crossed the street and headed toward them.

Carlo was dressed in the tweed jacket, turtleneck sweater, and slacks that were almost his uniform. His companion wore jeans, a slim-cut white shirt open at the neck and loafers without socks, his dark brown hair swept back into coarse, shaggy waves. He looked more like a graduate student than a colleague, obviously much younger than Carlo. His aviator sunglasses reflected Julia's image as she approached. She wondered if his research interest required him to blend in with the scene at local restaurants and bars.

"Julia, this is Rocco," Carlo said. Rocco shook her hand and helped her into a chair opposite him at the table. "Carlo has told me a great deal about you," he said after they were seated. "I understand you were a student here."

"Quite a while ago, yes," she laughed. "Carlo is a good friend from those days."

Rocco smiled. "Carlo has lots of friends among his former students." He paused, not one to bother with small talk. "He has also told me about your friend Robert. I gather he may have gotten himself into trouble."

Carlo had obviously given Rocco a summary of Robert's failed raid, so Julia filled in the details as best she could, sharing the rest of what Robert had told her. She stopped as their sandwiches and drinks were delivered to their table, and they began to eat. After the waiter had moved far enough away that he couldn't hear their conversation, she resumed her account.

Rocco interrupted her a few times with a couple of specific questions about how the raid was conducted. His main interest, however, was location. "Did he identify the building where they thought the sex slaves were being kept?"

"I really can't give you any more details," she said. "Not from what Robert told me. But a friend of mine in the *pensione* had an experience that might narrow down the location." She described the discovery and rescue of the two young girls by Amanda and Renzo in the basement beneath the tower complex.

After she had finished, Rocco shook his head. "Robert and his friends were stupid to assume they could expose that operation. Sex traffickers are professional criminals, vicious and cruel. And Robert and his friends are amateurs. They may mean well, but they're lucky they escaped with no more than some injuries. They could have been killed."

"Do you have any idea about who Robert might have been with?" Carlo asked.

"There's more than one group that has tried to take on the traffickers," Rocco answered. "The ones that work together with the police are safer. But if Robert is involved with a bunch that are trying to do this on their own, that's very risky."

They continued to eat in silence until Rocco suddenly remembered the other items Julia wanted to share. "Carlo tells me you have photos of a man you think has been stalking you. May I see them?"

Julia pulled the proof sheets out of her camera bag and handed them to him, pointing out in the first couple of shots the man in the T-shirt lurking in the background. He studied the images carefully. "I know a little bit about him," he said. "He's one of my intermediaries."

"That's why I couldn't tell you anything about him, Julia," Carlo interjected. "I figured that was up to Rocco."

Rocco nodded at Carlo and continued. "This guy hangs out a lot near the historic sites. He's a small-time crook who moves around on the fringes of the syndicates in town. He's been useful to me because I pay him."

"Why is he following me?"

"You may just have gotten in the way of someplace he wanted to be or someone he wanted to meet. Or he might have been afraid that you saw him doing something that he didn't want you to see. He walks a thin line—the way he crosses sides. So, he's too worried about his own safety to be a threat to anyone else. Attention is what he fears most. I don't think you need to worry about him."

Julia sighed and leaned back in her chair. Another possibility occurred to her. "Do you think he might have some connection to Robert and the raid?" she asked.

"I hope not. If he has information of interest to the syndicate, he might share it—for a price—with his contacts there."

Rocco could see how concerned Julia was about her friend. "Look," he said, "I can nose around and see what I can find out about him. If the raid Robert and his friends tried to pull off involved this guy, I'll let you know what I discover."

"Thank you! I would appreciate that."

"One more thing," he added, and pointed to the proof sheet Julia had shared with him. "There's a lot going on in several of these photos that may be important too."

Julia leaned forward and looked carefully at the images he pointed out. Two girls in a doorway, talking to an older gentleman, followed several steps behind by a younger man.

"Do you see what might be going on there?" he asked.

"Of course. They're prostitutes."

"If it's street prostitution, it could be legal. Or it might be trafficking. But they're pretty obviously soliciting. And the young guy is probably their protector. Or their pimp."

CHAPTER 32

Nic was waiting for Julia again. He had told Julia he would meet her at Paoli during his evening work break. *She's always late. I think she likes to make an entrance.* He was sitting at their favorite table on the side wall when she entered the restaurant accompanied by Amanda. Puzzled, he rose to greet both, leaning forward to kiss Julia on the cheek. After all three were seated, Julia reached out and patted his hand.

"So what's up?" he said, looking first at Amanda and then closely at Julia.

"Well, for one thing, I've seen Robert."

"Really? Where?" *Why is she so obsessed with him?* He couldn't conceal the edge in his voice at the mention of Robert.

"He came to see me. He was injured and needed a place to rest for a while."

"Injured? What happened?"

"He and a few of his friends were following some sort of lead about a sex trafficking operation. When they entered the place where they had been told it was located, they were attacked and beaten."

Nic frowned. His concern seemed genuine, so Julia decided to share more of what she knew. She described the raid Robert and his team had attempted and how they were ambushed when they entered the building where they had heard young women were being held captive.

"Is he still at your *pensione*?" Nic asked. "I want to talk to him." *And I want to find out what he has been up to.*

"No, he left yesterday morning. I don't know where he is now."

Nic's disappointment was obvious. He was quiet, processing what Julia had said.

Julia broke the silence. "I hope you don't mind that I asked Amanda to join us tonight. She may have another angle on the raid."

Nic turned to look at Amanda. "I think I've seen you around Florence," he said. "You're a tour guide, aren't you?"

"I was. Now I just come here on holiday."

Julia sensed more explanation was needed. "Amanda is staying at the *Pensione Europa*. That's how we met. She's the person I told you about—the one who has been checking out some of the tower neighborhoods."

Amanda was eager to share what she had discovered. She described what she and her friend Renzo had found beyond the basement of the building where his family's shop was located. Nic interrupted several times to ask her to clarify where they had been and how they got there. When she got to the part about their encounter with the two young girls who had fled from the sex trafficking operation, he reached in his pocket and pulled out a small notebook and pen. *She's on to something big.*

"Hold on," he said. "I hope you don't mind, but I'll need a record of what you're telling me."

Amanda nodded, waiting until Nic signaled he was ready, and then proceeding with the girls' account of their imprisonment and a description of how she and Renzo had rescued the two and found a safe place for them to stay.

"They're in a shelter now. I'm not sure where, but Renzo knows."

Nic closed his notebook and smiled. "I can't thank you enough, Amanda. This may be the break we've been hoping for."

"Break? In what?" Julia asked. She had hoped he would be interested in what Amanda had discovered, but she was surprised at his suggestion of its significance.

"We've known that some sort of trafficking was going on somewhere in that area, but we couldn't get any solid proof of what it was or where it was located. The operation has been too well concealed. Amanda has provided a tip that ties a lot of things together."

"Well, it looks like my work here is done," Amanda said, chuckling as she pushed her chair back and got ready to leave. "If you need more, you know where to find me."

"Don't go!" Julia said. "We'd love for you to enjoy dinner with us."

"Thanks, but no. I'm still tired from last night. I'm going to go back and enjoy dinner at the *Europa* and go to bed early for a change." She extended her hand to Nic. "It's a pleasure to meet you. I hope I've been of help. And I'll tell Renzo you'll be in touch with him."

Nic's reply was immediate and warm. *"Mi piacere.* I'll follow up with Renzo tomorrow."

Julia watched her friend wind her way around the

tables of the now-crowded restaurant. When Amanda was out the door, Julia moved from her chair opposite Nic and joined him on the banquette along the wall. He put his arm around her shoulders and drew her to him, kissing her on the forehead. "Now, let's talk about us," he said, smiling.

"Not so fast! I still have a couple of unanswered questions,"

"About what?"

"Well, for one thing, why didn't Robert's contact in the police department share with you what he was up to before the raid? Don't they stay in touch about such things?"

Nic looked around the restaurant before he answered, making sure no one was close enough to hear their conversation. *I should tell her. She needs to know.*

"Julia," he said in a voice just above a whisper, "I am Robert's contact in the department."

She gasped and leaned away from him. Before she could express her shock, Nic added quickly. "I know I should have told you this before, but things seemed under control until recently."

"What happened to change that?"

"Robert stopped checking in with me. He seemed to have found another source that he was depending on more. And he didn't like that I told him not to go after the sex traffickers on his own."

"Do you have any idea who the other source was?"

"No. I'm just pretty sure it wasn't anyone in the police department. And the fact that he and his friends were ambushed tells me they were betrayed by someone. Could have been his source. That's who would have known where they were going."

Julia was at a loss for words. She moved closer to Nic and leaned against his shoulder. "What can we do to help him?" she asked.

"Try to find out where he is so I can talk to him. And if you can have anything else—no matter how unrelated it might seem—I want you to share it with me."

She thought for a moment. "Actually, I have some photos. They're in my hotel room. I'll show them to you."

After dinner, they went back to the *Pensione Europa*. Nic stayed with Julia for as long as he could until he had to get back to work, taking a couple of the photos of the man in the black T-shirt with him when he left. "He looks familiar," he told her, "but I can't place him. He might just be a local who shows up a lot in tourist spots. I'll let you know what I find out."

He kissed Julia good night and threw her another kiss as he headed out the door.

CHAPTER 33

The passageways under the buildings of the tower complex didn't seem as daunting for Renzo as they had been when he and Amanda had explored them a couple of nights earlier. Maybe he was just used to their twists and turns now and knew where they would end. Or maybe it was because this time, he was with Officer Rossi, who cleared away some of the clutter impeding their progress as they moved slowly from one basement to another.

Amanda had come to his shop to let him know about Rossi's interest in the underground tunnels they had found, so he was ready when the policeman called. The space still posed problems for Renzo because of his size, and Officer Rossi, though leaner, was tall enough that he, too, had to squeeze and crouch through the narrowest sections of the passage. At last, the two men pushed through the door that led into the room where Renzo and Amanda had found the two young girls.

"It took us a while to get them out of here," Renzo told Nic. "They were pretty cold and scared. And they weren't wearing much clothing. The first thing we did was bring them some warm coats to wear."

Nic listened but he concentrated more on trying to determine their whereabouts. "Renzo, can you tell what buildings we passed through to get here? And where we are now?"

"I've wondered that myself," Renzo answered. "I've been down here a couple of times now, and I've tried to keep track of how many foundations there are and how many tunnels."

"So what do you think?"

"We are no longer in the tower complex where my family's business is located. I think we've found a network of passageways that nobody has known about or used for centuries. And I think we're now underneath another complex."

Nic looked around the room, studying it carefully. *It looks like it may have been a storage area.* Turning to Renzo, he asked, "Where did the girls say they had entered? If we know that, we'll know how to get access to wherever they were being held hostage."

"They told us they found their way through crawl spaces leading away from a cellar of some sort. There's a hole in the wall over there," Renzo said, pointing.

Nic walked across the room and looked closely at the opening. "It's too narrow for most adults. That's probably why the girls weren't followed. But it does look big enough for children or small women."

Using a small flashlight he had brought with him, he leaned on the wall, shining the light into the darkness behind it. "I'm pretty sure they could have gotten here this way," he said in a muffled voice. "It opens up a little farther behind the wall, but they still wouldn't have been pursued by anyone bigger than them."

He stood and put the flashlight back in his pocket. "It's good that you and Amanda found them when you did. I don't see any way they could have gotten out."

Renzo gasped. "They would have died?"

Nic nodded. "Unless they were desperate enough to go back up into the place they left. And that would have been dangerous for them, too." He brushed the dirt off his suit. "I think I've seen enough to get an idea of what you found here. Thanks, Renzo. My next stop will be the shelter. I'll need to talk to the girls."

"Do you have to? They were very afraid and lost. And they don't want to do anything that would endanger their families back home."

"They won't have to testify when we bring the traffickers to trial. But if they give us information that helps us locate the building where they were held captive, we can do a police raid and arrest those running the operation."

"What about the other girls being held there? Will they be hurt?"

"No. Of course not. Our goal will be to rescue them and bring them out safely."

On their way back through the underground passageway to Renzo's shop, Nic took out the notebook and pen he carried with him and began to write.

"What are you doing?" Renzo asked, impatient with spending so much time in a narrow space that was making him feel uncomfortable again.

"I'm keeping track of how many basements we are passing through." Nic replied. "That will help me figure out at street level where we ended up. And what building the girls came from when they made their escape." He stopped and checked the small compass on his keychain. "And this tells me the directions the passageways follow."

It had taken longer than Renzo had anticipated to show Nic what he and Amanda had discovered, but once he was back in his shop, he felt both relieved and satisfied. "I hope this has been helpful:" he said to Nic as they shook hands.

"Renzo, you've given me very valuable information. Thank you."

"Enough to capture and arrest the men who were holding those young girls captive? What they did was awful."

"I hope so, Renzo. I hope so."

Nic left Renzo's shop and headed to the shelter, more determined than ever. *When we find the bastards, I hope we can make them pay for what they're doing.*

The assault team was assembled quickly, aided by the new information Nic had gathered about the building where he suspected the girls were held captive. Using the notes he had taken while he and Renzo explored the passages leading from Renzo's shop, it hadn't taken long for him to determine where they led. It was a simple calculation, confirmed by his brief interview with the young girls in the shelter. He had retraced the route at street level, arriving at a commercial building that appeared to be vacant, awaiting a scheduled renovation. *I wonder if the owners even know what is going on here?*

Luigi, the leader of the team, started by testing the door at the side of the building. It was locked, so he kicked at the middle of the panel. The wood was old and splintered easily. He broke through and, together with the rest of his squad, raced up the stairs that led to the upper floors of the building.

Several men dressed in black trousers and short-sleeved shirts ran out of a room at the top of the stairway and started toward Luigi and his fellow officers. "We're the police!" Luigi shouted, drawing his gun. "And you're under arrest."

The traffickers weren't about to give up easily. Young and muscular, they lunged at the policemen, swinging their fists and attempting to wrestle the guns away from Luigi and his men. The battle didn't last long. The police squad was twice the size of the group attacking them and just as strong. Within minutes, they had their targets pinned to the floor.

Nic Rossi came up the stairs in time to see Luigi and the others handcuffing the men they were arresting. Behind them, a long corridor led away from the stairway and opened on to a row of rooms, out of which young women, most of them in their early teens, were now poking their heads and watching with fear-filled eyes.

"You'll be okay," he said to them, his voice deliberately quiet and reassuring. "We'll take you to a place where you'll be safe and away from all this." Reaching into his pocket, he pulled out his *telefonino* to summon the female officers waiting outside the building. "Everything's under control up here," he said. "You can come and help the girls."

Piero Manca loved his early evening stroll home after he finished his shift in the hotel bar. Especially at this time of year. Summer was approaching, and the days were warmer, daylight lasting longer. He lingered a moment just outside the front door of the hotel and breathed deeply. The aroma of veal simmering in a tasty meat broth and white wine sauce wafted his way from somewhere close by. Maybe one of the restaurants in the next block. And flowers. He could smell the scent of flowers too.

Heading out of the *piazzetta*, down the short alley leading to the bustling streets of the adjacent neighborhood, he paused. Which direction should he take to go to his apartment? The long way home or the shorter route? The longer route, he decided. It was such a beautiful evening.

As he rounded the corner leading to the businesses near the tourist sites, he stopped, startled by what he saw. Several vehicles were gathered to the side of one of the buildings—one that, he recalled from previous walks in the neighborhood, had seemed unoccupied or at least lacking any clear commercial purpose. Several policemen were hustling a group of handcuffed young men out of the building and forcing them into the police cruisers. Behind them, still in the shadow of the alley along the side entry of the building, was a cluster of young girls huddled close to a couple of policewomen who had draped coats around their shoulders.

A crowd of onlookers was gathered on the narrow sidewalk across the street from the building, watching all that was going on. Piero strolled up to a woman observing the action, her face reflecting the horror she was feeling. From the fashionable style of her dress and the colorful scarf looped around her neck, he could tell she was Florentine. "What's going on?" he asked in Tuscan dialect to set her at ease in case she didn't want to share her concerns with a tourist.

"Some sort of rescue of women held inside that place,"

she answered, pointing at the building. "They've already brought a lot of them out." She paused and sighed. "They looked so young—and so frightened."

"Trafficking, maybe?" Piero asked. The woman nodded. Many citizens of Florence had heard rumors about a local sex trade, even if they didn't know much else about where it was located or how it operated.

Piero thought back to the scene he had witnessed in the alley near the hotel the night he was attacked. The building where he saw the suspicious behavior wasn't far from this one. *Could they be connected?*

The police cars carrying the men in handcuffs slowly moved down the street while the procession of young girls out of the building came to a close, too. Several female officers helped them into vans waiting in the alley and then closed the doors and climbed into the front seats. As those vehicles left the scene, two more policemen exited the building and fastened the shattered door behind them. One of them walked toward the spectators gathered on the sidewalk.

Piero recognized him. It was Niccolo Rossi, the officer who had overseen the investigation of the attack on him.

Rossi was met with a barrage of questions shouted at him.

"What's going on, officer?"

"What will happen to the girls? Were they arrested too?"

The questions kept coming so quickly that Piero had trouble hearing specific ones. So, apparently, did Officer Rossi. He waved his hand, calling for silence, and calmly spoke. "I'm afraid there's nothing I can tell you. This is a police matter. It's all over, so you might as well be on your way. But I can assure you, everything is safe here now."

The crowd of onlookers slowly dispersed, muttering as they headed in several directions away from the scene. Piero stayed long enough for Officer Rossi to notice him. He had told Rossi during the investigation of the attack on him that he was certain that he had stumbled on a situation involving the kidnapping of young girls.

"Officer Rossi!" he called out. "The building I was checking out?" alluding to the suspicions he already held. He knew Rossi would understand what he was asking.

Nic nodded and put a finger to his lips, signaling that he couldn't or wouldn't say more. Piero nodded back. It was a confidence they shared, and he would honor it.

Returning to his usual route home, he felt relieved and happier than he had felt in the long weeks that had followed his attack. It all made sense now. He had wandered into a place where he had come too close to a sex-trafficking operation and had been beaten up for it. It wasn't just a random encounter. The assault on him may even have given the police a clue about crimes that they were now able to expose and criminals they were able to arrest.

So he had done some good. He hadn't just made a silly mistake. Even better, he thought, he was in on a secret.

Smiling, entering the busy piazza that opened out from the street where he had been walking, he joined the throng of tourists and workers bustling their way to their destinations for the evening. The approach of the millennium and anticipation of the Great Jubilee were bringing even more visitors to Florence than usual. The streets were packed.

Piero couldn't help himself. He felt like whistling. So he did, much to the annoyance of everyone around him.

CHAPTER 34

Robert and his friends were still in the doctor's house, lounging on chairs and sofas in the library. They had been encamped there for three days, more than the doctor promised when they first arrived, but necessary, everyone felt, for their safety. Their wounds were healing. Even Giuseppe was recovered enough to join them in the library.

Sandro's *telefonino* rang. He rose to take the call, standing close to the window where the reception was best. The others listened anxiously to his end of the conversation. "Yes. Yes. When did it happen?" A long pause, and he smiled. "Fantastic!" he exclaimed.

He closed the phone and turned to look at his friends, beaming as he shared with them the information he had just received. "The police raided the building where we were trying to rescue the girls!" he exclaimed. "They've made some arrests!"

Robert and the others leaped to their feet, laughing as they exchanged high fives. Finally, there was a victory for their cause. Even better, it would bring an end to their isolation and confinement.

"So, what's next?" Sandro asked as they sat down again, facing each other. There was still the threat that their group might be targeted again, they realized. From what his phone contact had told Sandro, the ring that had arranged the attack on their friends in front of the Duomo was also the one that had been raided and arrested. But they might be less dangerous now, at least for a while.

"They have other things to worry about," Giuseppe said. "They're not likely to call attention to themselves by attacking us or anyone else in the city."

"I think you're right," the doctor agreed. "They'll have to lie low."

"And so should we," Robert said. "If the police are aware of the problem and are taking action."

"But we need to report back to the rest of the group about what happened to us," Sandro insisted. "And we still don't know who tipped off the goons who attacked us. Our work is still in danger until we figure that out."

"I think we need to go home first," Antonio said. He was the oldest on their team. His opinion mattered. "Let the police do the rest of the work they need to do. Maybe then things will be clearer."

Robert nodded in agreement. "For now, I just want to sleep in my own bed. Anyway, I think I know who betrayed us. We can figure out later how to deal with him."

Later that night, over dinner at Paoli, sitting next to each other at their favorite table along the side wall, Nic shared with Julia a few details of the raid. He couldn't tell her everything, he said. The men arrested would be brought to trial eventually, and until then facts about them and the place where they were found had to be protected. But his obvious relief showed in what he told her.

"We've pretty much shut down that operation. And we've picked up some other useful leads through the phone records of a couple of the men we arrested."

"Leading to what?" Julia asked.

"Other sites where women are being victimized. Massage parlors. Apartments. Some with ties to drug trafficking. They're all connected, as it turns out, at least in this ring."

"You mean there are others?"

"Unfortunately, yes. With links to other countries and crime syndicates. This is a huge problem internationally, Julia. We can only hope to expose and stamp out a few operations at a time."

Julia sighed and rested her head on Nic's shoulder. "This is so depressing. Amanda and I were talking about this the other day. For all the hope we had that things might have gotten better for women since the days of women's prisons, it seems they're just as bad now, but in a different way."

"For some, yes. But police and government agencies are beginning to see how big the problem is. Maybe that will lead to change."

"What about the girls?" she asked, raising her head and looking at Nic. "What will happen to them?"

"They're at the shelter. They'll be fed and given a safe place to stay. And taken care of for a while. Most likely, they'll eventually be returned to their homes."

"I know about the shelters. Amanda told me a little about the safe havens they provide, but why should the girls be sent back home afterward? They came here for a better life, to get away from conditions where they lived before."

"True, but obviously they didn't find the better life they were looking for, did they? They don't have the means to do something else here, so they'll be better off back where they came from."

Julia shook her head and sighed again. "It's all so sad and complicated. "

Nic put his arm around her shoulder and drew her to him, kissing her on her cheek. "Can we talk about us now?"

She smiled. "Yes! I want to think about things that make me happy."

CHAPTER 35

Amanda was packed and ready for her return home and wanted to spend her last day in Florence sightseeing with Julia. They had breakfast together in the dining room, to plan their itinerary. "I come to Florence every year to see the places that mean the most to me." Amanda said. "And every year, at the end of my holiday, I try to see as many of them as I can one more time."

"What makes them special? I mean, you've led tours in other Italian cities. There's beautiful art and important history there, too. Why Florence?"

"Because this is where it all began." She hesitated. It was clear the story she was about to tell was difficult for her. "I haven't shared this with you before, but I have a deep personal tie to Florence."

"Take your time, Amanda," Julia said softly. "You don't have to tell me anything if it's hard for you."

Amanda sat straighter in her chair and looked directly at Julia. "No, it's something I want you to know about me.

You see, I married young. Right after I graduated from university. But Tony, my husband, died in an automobile accident a few months after our wedding."

"Oh, Amanda, I'm so sorry."

"Don't fret, Julia. That was a long time ago. And my life definitely changed. Tony will always be in my heart, but I didn't want to continue on the path I had shared with him. He was from an old family. Old money. He left me comfortably fixed for life. After I lost him, I needed something entirely different. I just wanted to get away from England. So I came to Florence on holiday. To escape reality, in a way."

"Only to Florence?"

"Oh, no, it was supposed to be more of a grand tour. But I loved Florence so much I extended my stay here. I had taken some art history classes at the university and certain sites and collections of art really spoke to me. I decided I wanted a career and a way of life that allowed me to come back and see them over and over again."

"Did you have any regrets? I mean, that was such a big change for you."

"Not about the career. It was a good choice. I've loved every minute of it." She paused. "My only regret is that Tony and I didn't have children."

Julia was quiet. It was clear Amanda had more to say.

I think maybe that's why I'm so upset by what had been done to the young girls Renzo and I found. Children should be protected and treasured, not abused."

Amanda kept picking at her food before she spoke again. "Now you know why this trip every year is so important to me."

"It's kind of a personal pilgrimage for you, isn't it?"

Amanda smiled sadly and nodded. "Yes. And a way of

remembering Tony." Her voice was husky. "Today I will be promising to myself that I will return. Sharing it with you will make it even more special."

"I'm honored! Where do we start?"

Amanda folded her napkin and placed it alongside her empty plate. She was all business again. "Let's wrap up the matter of the young girls first. We'll stop by Renzo's shop and tell him about the raid. He'll be happy to know the traffickers were arrested."

Renzo had already heard the news. "That's not exactly the kind of thing that goes unnoticed in the neighborhood," he said. "Word of the arrests spread pretty quickly. But what I want to know is, what will happen to the girls?"

"Nic couldn't—or wouldn't—say," Julia answered. "He thinks they will probably be kept for a while at the shelter so their wounds can heal and they can get some counseling. But they may have to be sent home."

Amanda was leaning on the glass counter where Renzo's elegant leather gloves were arrayed. She was listening carefully to Julia. "That's not fair!" she exclaimed. "Home probably isn't a better life for them. Otherwise, they wouldn't have left, would they?"

Julia nodded. "I agree. But Nic says what are their prospects here? They have no money, no place to stay, and they're not trained for any meaningful kind of work."

Amanda stepped away from the counter, shaking her head. "Maybe. It just breaks my heart."

"Same here. But there's nothing we can do about it, unfortunately. Renzo, is there some chance I could see the shelter you took the girls to? Amanda told me a little about it."

"Maybe later. After we know the girls are safely someplace else. I promised I wouldn't disclose anything until then."

Disappointed, Julia decided not to press the issue. Instead, she looked around at the collection of other leather goods in Renzo's shop. They were obviously of very high quality —much better than she had seen elsewhere. "Renzo," she said impulsively. "I've been shopping for a wallet. May I see what you have?"

"With pleasure!" Renzo smiled. "Gabriela will help you. She is my very able assistant."

Julia walked over to the section where wallets and purses were displayed while Amanda and Renzo continued to chat with each other. It was clear the two were old friends with a special relationship, and she wanted to give them time alone.

Gabriela brought out trays of wallets and placed them on the counter for Julia to examine more closely. They were all beautifully crafted. "I can't make up my mind," Julia smiled at the young clerk, who smiled back. She settled on a black flap wallet in an exquisitely smooth black leather. Gabriela wrapped it in tissue paper and placed it in a small plastic bag embossed with the logo for Renzo's shop.

Julia turned to see if her friend was ready to leave. Renzo was looking sad. He leaned forward and kissed Amanda on the cheek.

"Come back soon," he said.

"I will. I already have my reservations for later this year." Amanda patted his hand and turned to signal to Julia that she was ready to leave.

"Let's start with the first site that left me gobsmacked," she said as she and Julia walked out the door of Renzo's shop, down the street toward the Duomo. Wrapping the scarf around her head and tying it, she buttoned her tweed jacket. She was the image of a tour guide, ready to share tidbits of Florentine history and gossip.

They stopped at the east door of the Baptistery with its "Gate of Paradise" panels facing the cathedral. Amanda paused for a moment. "These blew me away—their artistry and the story of the competition that produced him. And the same thing happened when I saw the other Baptistery doors and the wooden statue of *la madallena*—the penitent Mary Magdalene—inside. I couldn't get over them."

She pointed at the Museo dell' Opera del Duomo on the other side of the piazza. "These panels are copies, as you know. The originals are in the museum over there. And so is the Mary Magdalene."

"Do you want to visit the museum?"

"No. This is the spot that first spoke to me so powerfully. I like to remember that moment." *What would Tony have thought of my obsession with Florence? How different would my life have been if he had lived?*

Amanda took a tissue from her pocket and wiped a tear from her eye. After a moment, she waved her hand at Julia. "Come on. I want to spend some time at the Bargello. And there's something amusing I want you to see along the way."

Strolling down the Via del Corso, they turned down a narrow street and passed the Casa di Dante, a place Julia remembered visiting in her student days. Built on the site of Dante's family home, the small museum contained a collection of his works and other pieces documenting his life. But that wasn't Amanda's destination. They walked a bit farther and arrived at an ancient church tucked between two other buildings on a nearby street.

"This is one of the oldest neighborhoods in Florence, and this was the family church for the woman who became Dante's wife," she whispered as they stepped inside. "I found it utterly charming on my first visit to Florence. I still do." She paused and looked around. "They were married here. One legend says this is also where he first saw Beatrice."

"The Beatrice who was the inspiration for one of his guides in The Divine Comedy?" Julia asked. "I read that in a literature course I took my sophomore year."

"One and the same. Whether or not that legend is true, her family did worship here, and this is where she is buried. She died young."

It was just a small parish church, clearly very old. Near the exit was a basket filled with notes. Amanda pointed to it and smiled. "This is what I wanted you to see. If you need advice on your love life, you can leave a message for Beatrice here."

Julia laughed and then lowered her voice as the other two tourists in the church turned to look at her. "I'll keep that in mind. I may be back."

A few blocks away, they approached the Bargello. "This used to be a prison," Julia said, contemplating the sturdy fortress and austere stone facade.

"Yes. A city hall first and then police headquarters and a prison before it was finally turned into a museum. It's the oldest public building in Florence. Given your fascination with the Pazzi attack on Giuliano Medici in the Duomo, you probably know that some of the assassins were executed here."

"Yes. I remember reading about one of them. As I

recall, after the execution, his body was hung from a window as a lesson to anyone else who might try to do the same thing. I have to admit that image is the first thing I think of whenever I visit the Bargello."

"He wasn't the only one. The same thing happened at the Palazzo Vecchio. Men executed and hung from the windows. And some were hunted down and killed by mobs."

"That was such a brutal time. This is where the violence of that era seems most real to me. There were so many rivals to Medici rule, weren't there?"

Amanda kept talking as they entered the courtyard and headed up the stairs to the Upper Loggia. "The Pazzi are the best known. Their family was banished from Florence after Giuliano was assassinated. The Strozzi were rivals too, although they alternated between being allies and enemies. In fact, many powerful families in Florence were jealous of Medici power. Not surprising, really. Their influence lasted more or less continuously over 300 years."

"Were the Medici so awful?"

"No worse than most during those times. There were some good ones among them. Lorenzo the Magnificent especially."

They had reached the Donatello Room and Amanda was eager to see the artist's bronze statue of David. As she gazed at the elegant figure, she offered one more observation about the culture that had produced such masterpieces. "All the rivalries back then were mainly about money and power. Isn't that always the case?"

Julia nodded. "It's the same today. Except the challengers now seem to be crime rings and syndicates. I've found it interesting on this trip that people can't help comparing modern contenders to the Medici and their opponents."

"Sad but true," Amanda said, leaning forward to study the Donatello masterpiece more closely. And then she straightened up and looked at her watch. "I can't believe I'm already getting hungry. Once we finish up here, we can have lunch."

CHAPTER 36

Julia convinced her friend to dine at a restaurant near Santa Croce rather than back at the *pensione*. "It'll be my treat, Amanda. You've made me feel so much at home during my stay. And besides, I owe you some sort of commission for helping to solve the mystery of the sex trafficking operations near my old hotel."

Amanda laughed. "We were pretty good detectives, weren't we?" Over their meals, reminiscing about the adventure they had shared, she paused for a moment. "Will I see you the next time I come to Florence?"

Julia shrugged. "That depends on when you will be here."

"But won't you be staying here? Living here by then?"

"What are you getting at?"

"Well, it's clear you and Nic are pretty serious about each other. You aren't going to give that up just to go back to the States, are you?"

Julia hesitated, trying to sort out her feelings before responding. "I honestly don't know, Amanda. That would be a big change in my life. I'm not sure I'm ready for it."

"At least give it a try, Julia. If you don't, I think you'll regret it."

Julia studied the expression on Amanda's face. "Are you thinking about yourself and Renzo?"

Amanda poked at the plate of pasta in front of her. "In a way, yes. I am," she replied. "Renzo has been a great comfort to me. But my love of Tony has always stood between us."

Their conversation stopped. The waiter brought their second course, and they ate in silence until Julia looked across the table and said, "Tell you what. After we finish eating, it'll be my turn to show you some of the places in Florence that have special meaning for me—over on the Oltrarno."

"The Pitti Palace? Santo Spirito?"

"No. A neighborhood close to them. I used to live there."

"With your parents?"

"With my fiancé."

Amanda's eyes widened. "Really? The plot has begun to thicken. When was that? And who was that?"

With Amanda listening intently, Julia shared the story about her relationship with Bill, including the way it ended. By the time she finished, the waiter had cleared away their dishes, and they were enjoying the last sips of the wine they had ordered. Julia's mood had turned pensive. "Sorry, I'm getting a little emotional," she said. "I thought I was over it. I guess I'm not."

Amanda reached across the table and patted her hand. "Young love. First love. That's the one you never forget." *I know I will never forget Tony.* She looked away for a moment and then leaned back in her chair, contemplating the secret Julia had entrusted her with. "You've told me that your return to Florence had a personal dimension. I assumed it was your childhood here with your parents. Was it actually about your life with Bill?"

"Both. I did want to come back because even though I have such fond memories of my early years in Florence, I don't remember them very clearly. That's also why I signed up for a study abroad experience when I was in college. But this time, it's also about confronting my memories of Bill and putting them behind me."

"Have you succeeded?"

"I thought I had, until just now, when I started to share things with you. Some of it came rushing back."

Amanda waited, not wanting to ask a question that would upset Julia even more. "Is that why you're having trouble committing to a deeper relationship with Nic?"

Julia stared at Amanda and took a moment to answer. "Probably."

"Then let's go over to the neighborhood you knew with Bill. Sometimes it just helps to confront your memories and talk them through. Get them off your chest."

They wandered first through the area Bill had chosen as his home before Julia moved in with him. She pointed out the apartment building. "It was on the second floor. Nothing special. But it was furnished. Good enough to stay in for a few months."

The next stop, a few blocks away, was the trattoria where she and Bill had enjoyed special meals together. Its simple decor suggested it was aimed more at a neighborhood clientele than at the tourist trade. A few tables were set up on a terrace in front, and beaded curtains led to a small dining area inside.

"Bill proposed to me here. It looks pretty much the

same as it did then." She paused. "That seems such a long time ago now."

"Does it bother you to see it again, when it has such special memories?"

Julia shook her head. "Sort of. But not really, if that makes any sense. Seeing all this just reminds me of what happened after we left Italy and returned to the States and how I felt then. That's what I wanted to put behind me."

"That's a start. Remember the whole story, not just the beginning. It puts things in perspective."

"I'm glad we came here today. It reminds me that I'm a much different person now." She walked a few paces more and stared at the trattoria. "You know what's ironic? Nic's apartment is in this neighborhood too." She shrugged. "I guess I can't escape this place no matter how my life has changed."

She looked around at the featureless stone buildings surrounding the piazza where they stood. Finally, she turned to Amanda and linked arms with her. "I've seen enough, Amanda. Let's get on with our sightseeing."

Walking back over the Ponte Vecchio, they decided to spend the rest of the afternoon visiting places with art pieces that Amanda particularly liked. The major museums were still closed, and so were many of the churches, so they had some time to kill. Enough to take care of an errand.

"I want to check at the railway station to make sure the time for the departure of my train to Milano hasn't changed," Amanda said as they strolled toward the city center. "After I get that, we can stop by Santa Maria Novella. I want to see Ghirlandaio's frescoes."

The station was busy as usual, packed with crowds of travelers. Amanda took her place in line at the information booth where timetables were available, patiently waiting her turn. "This shouldn't take too long," she told Julia.

"That's okay. I think I'll check out that chocolate and gelato shop we saw on our way in."

When Julia emerged into the piazza with two boxes of chocolates, Amanda was heading toward her with a timetable in hand. "Is that for us?" she laughed, pointing at the candy.

"Why not? We deserve something to celebrate the day. Are you ready to leave?"

"I am." Amanda waved the timetable before she put it in her purse. "Let's go see the frescoes. We'll even have time to visit San Lorenzo before dinner."

Suddenly, there were shouts and a commotion coming from the street where they were headed. At a distance, they saw a man in a hooded sweatshirt and black trousers racing toward the station entrance, careening wildly as he swerved to avoid passengers burdened with their luggage. Looking desperately from side to side, he appeared to be trying to find a place to hide or escape.

He bumped into two elderly tourists who were moving slowly, burdened by their luggage, almost knocking them down. The shouts grew louder. "Watch out! What's your hurry? Be careful!"

"This is crazy," Amanda said. "Let's get out of here." They walked across the piazza, toward the church of Santa Maria Novella and were greeted by the same priest who had been so helpful to Julia at the beginning of her photo shoot. He recognized her.

"*Signorina!* It is nice to see you again. You were working on an article about the millennium, right? How did it turn out?"

"Very well, thanks to you. I followed your advice and focused on people, not just on buildings."

The priest beamed and bowed his head slightly. "I'm so glad I could be of help. Has it been published?"

"Not yet, but it will be. My editor likes what he has seen so far. I'll make sure you get a copy when it comes out."

The priest clapped his hands and his smile broadened. "Thank you! And what brings you here today?"

Julia pointed toward Amanda. "My friend needed to stop by the train station. And now we're eager to see the chapels and the frescoes here."

"This is a good time of the afternoon to see them. I'll leave you to enjoy your visit." He waved and turned to greet other tourists who had entered the piazza.

Amanda and Julia headed to the Tornabuoni Chapel. Amanda was describing her reaction the first time she saw the frescoes there when the quiet tranquility of their surroundings was broken by the wail of police and ambulance sirens outside. Within minutes, the priest came scurrying into the church and sought them out. "It might not be a good time for you to be here," he said breathlessly. "Something serious seems to have happened at the station. Lots of emergency vehicles just drove by and the police have started to set up barriers at the edge of our piazza to keep people from going down the street."

"What on earth could have happened?" Julia said, looking around to see how other tourists in the church were reacting.

"Probably just an accident," the priest suggested.

"Or an assault of some sort," Amanda added sharply. *He doesn't want to give the impression that a place so close to the church can be dangerous.*

The priest shrugged his shoulders. "I'll go talk to the police at the barriers. Maybe they can tell me what's going on." He turned and hurried away from them again.

"What should we do now?"

"We can go to San Lorenzo for a while to see the Medici tombs. We'll come back here if there's time."

Their visit at San Lorenzo was spent wandering through the basilica, but Julia couldn't stop wondering about what had happened at the train station. "I'm having trouble concentrating," she said.

"So am I," Amanda confessed. "I keep thinking the accident, or whatever it was, must have involved that man who was behaving so strangely."

"Same with me. I'm really curious. I didn't see his face, but he seemed very familiar. And I don't remember seeing anyone chasing him, do you?"

"It was so crowded in the station, I didn't notice."

"Well, let's go back to Santa Maria Novella to see if anything has changed."

As they approached, they could see that the police barrier was still up.

"I have an idea," Julia said. "Let's check with the priest to see if he heard anything new while we were gone."

The priest was excited to share what he had been told by the police guarding the street outside the church piazza. "A man fell onto the tracks and one of the trains ran over him. It was a pretty bloody accident."

"Run over by a train? How did that happen?"

"Apparently, he was running very fast and stumbled. He landed on a track as a train was arriving. It couldn't stop in time to avoid hitting him."

"It sounds like it may have been the same guy we saw. That's awful."

Amanda grabbed Julia by the arm. "I don't want to hang around here anymore. We might get stuck in a police investigation. Let's go back to the *pensione* and have some wine before dinner." Nodding goodbye to the priest, she pulled Julia with her.

This isn't the way I wanted the last day of my vacation to end.

CHAPTER 37

Julia got up early to join Amanda for breakfast before the cab arrived to pick her up. As they had over dinner the night before, they avoided talking about the unpleasant scene at the train station. They spent most of their time comparing opinions about their favorite places in Florence. And laughing about their first impressions of each other.

"Miss Marple?" Amanda asked with mock indignation.

"Lucy Honeychurch?" Julia gasped.

"Of course. She couldn't make up her mind either about the man in her life."

"Too true. But she was British, so it doesn't fit me exactly, does it?"

"Close enough!" Amanda said, laughing.

When the time came for Amanda to leave, Julia helped her take her luggage down to the street where the cab was waiting. "You have my address, so promise me you'll stay in touch," Amanda said.

"I will," Julia nodded. "And be sure to let me know

when you'll be in Florence again. If I'm here...I'll want to see you."

The cab driver placed Amanda's luggage in the trunk. She turned and hugged Julia. "Remember what I told you about Nic," she said, and got into the back seat of the cab. Julia waved goodbye as the car pulled away and headed slowly down the narrow street. *I'm going to miss her*, she thought. *She's like a favorite aunt—but a lot more fun.*

Once upstairs, she stopped by the reception area of the *pensione*. A copy of the morning newspaper would be there by now. Leafing through it, she found a report of the accident at the train station on an inside page. Just a brief story with a small headline. A man running recklessly along one of the platforms had bumped into someone and stumbled onto the track of an arriving train. Killed instantly, his identity unknown.

Bumped into someone? Hard enough to fall off the platform? Why did that sound a bit suspicious? She decided to ask Nic if he knew anything about the accident when they had dinner that night.

Robert slept late. It was the first night he had spent in his apartment for a long time. Things just seemed too risky leading up to the raid, and after it failed, he thought he might have become a target for the syndicate running the sex trafficking ring. His source had told him that the criminals running the operation were aware of the plan his group had made to free the girls being held captive as sex slaves, and somehow they also knew the identity of those who were assigned to carry out the plan. But how? Relationships in the group were founded on trust and a belief that no one would violate their confidence or share their secrets.

He took his time getting ready for what might be a busy day. Lingering in the shower, he let the water flow over the cuts and bruises on his face. They had begun to heal, but they were soothed even more by the warmth of the spray. He didn't shave—that might have reopened some of the wounds. Looking at himself in the bathroom mirror as he toweled himself dry, he sized up the image he would be presenting to the world. *I like it. Rugged and sexy.*

Dressed casually and comfortably in slacks and a polo shirt, he made himself a pot of espresso. He carried a cup of the coffee and a couple of the breakfast croissants the doctor had sent home with him out onto the small balcony outside his apartment. Placing his breakfast meal on the table there, he settled onto a cushioned patio chair and leaned back to enjoy the view and the sounds of everyday activity in his neighborhood. People strolling down the sidewalk, chatting. A dog barking somewhere nearby. A small child's laughter as her mother called out to her.

Will I ever again be able to believe in the innocence of life in Florence now that I've seen the dark side?

The only way to hang on to that hope, he sensed, was to end his entanglement in the seamier aspects of Florentine existence. But first, he needed to be assured that those responsible for the crimes that were staining all that was good in Florence were brought to justice. And he wanted to expose the treachery of the confidante he had relied on for information about the sex trade in the city. He was pretty sure it was his source who had betrayed him and his team by tipping off the men who were running the trafficking operation.

I guess my only choice is to go back to see Nic Rossi. He had cut off that connection abruptly because the policeman had refused to support his plan to get more involved in investigations of sex traffickers. That was the initial reason for their split. And then it became personal. Sandro had seen Nic and Julia at Paoli and at concerts around town. "They're obviously more than just friends," Sandro had said.

Double-crossing S.O.B. He moves in on her when he knows I'm not around for a while.

As for Julia, she had hurt him once again, just as she had when she became involved with Bill during her year in Florence. He had hoped to win her back this time around. But now....

Nic was reviewing reports of the death at the train station when Robert tapped on the open door of his office to get his attention. He rose and motioned toward the chair opposite him at his desk.

"Robert! I'm glad to see you again. Have a seat."

As Robert settled into the chair, Nic looked at the bruises still showing on his face. "Are you sure those injuries are only superficial? Has someone checked them out?"

"I've seen a doctor. He says they're nothing serious. I'm already feeling better."

"Robert, I hate to say it, but the raid you and your friends tried to pull off was a very dangerous thing to do. You're lucky you weren't killed."

Robert stiffened in his chair. "How do you know about the raid?"

"Julia told me."

There it was, out in the open: Nic's relationship with

Julia. Robert narrowed his eyes and clenched his jaw. "If we're going to get anywhere in this conversation, you'd better not bring Julia into it." He glared at Nic.

Nic took a deep breath and waved his hand at Robert, calming him. "All right. We won't go there. I just wanted you to know that she's worried about you. But what did happen? And what brings you here today?"

"My team and I have heard about the police sweep of the building where we tried to free the young women. And we know there were arrests. We don't plan to do anything more to try to expose the sex trade in the city."

Nic nodded, relieved.

Robert continued. "What I want to know is who betrayed us. Who tipped off the sex traffickers so they knew we were coming? If it was someone in our own group, we need to warn the others."

"Do you have any suspicions about who it might have been?"

"If it wasn't a member of our group, it may have been my source. The guy who was supplying me with information about criminal activities in the city, the one who gave us some tips about what was going on in that building."

"And who was that?"

"He never told me his name. But he's pretty noticeable in the neighborhoods. Always dresses in black." He hesitated. "Julia saw him near the *Torrevecchia*. She thought he was following her."

Nic's answer came after a long pause. "I think I know who you're talking about. But you're not going to get any information from him."

"Why not? Can't you help me?"

"Not with this, Robert. That man is dead."

Robert leaned back in his chair and stared at Nic, his

jaw open in dismay. "Dead? As of when? I saw him a couple of days ago."

"Yesterday. He was run over by a train at Santa Maria Novella station."

"An accident?"

"That's what we are investigating. I can't say any more. But I want you to tell me everything you know about him. Where he hung out. With whom. And what kind of information he was giving you."

Nic ordered panini and drinks delivered to his office, so he and Robert could continue to talk uninterrupted.

"How did you meet the guy?" Nic asked as he took a bite out of his sandwich.

"The first time was after I dropped Julia off at the *Pensione Europa*. Her story about being followed by a man who seemed to be threatening her made me angry. I wanted to find him and beat him to a pulp."

Nic looked puzzled. "You were that angry? Why?"

Robert glared at him. "Because I care deeply for Julia. And I admit I feel protective of her. I could tell she was very frightened. The thought of someone wanting to harm her...."

"I understand," Nic said, concentrating on the notes he was taking of their conversation. He wasn't going to let this turn into a discussion of Julia. "So where did you find him?"

"I went back to the hotel where she had been staying and parked my car in the piazza in front of it. It was late, so there wasn't anyone else there. Pretty soon I saw him creeping out of a passageway close to the hotel, near the vacant warehouse. I got out of my car and followed him. When I caught up to him, I shoved him against the wall."

"And? Didn't he fight back?"

"No," Robert answered with a sneer. "He just started blubbering. Said he had seen some young women being pulled into the alley alongside the building, and he wanted to help them. But they were already inside and the door was locked."

"You believed him?"

"Not the whole story. But it seemed to confirm what you had told me in one of our earlier conversations—that you suspected there were some illegal operations going on in that neighborhood. I thought it was worth finding out more from him."

Nic was taking notes on Robert's report. "Was that the only information you got from him? How did that lead to the raid you tried to pull off?"

"We met a couple of times after that. At a bar. He said you can get into and out of the warehouse by way of the rooftop garden in the hotel. He did it once when he was trying to escape from someone he suspected was following him. Once he was on the warehouse roof, he could see through the skylight that girls were being held in an upper area of the building. He also told me that he had learned that members of the crime ring running the trafficking operations had stabbed our two friends in front of the Duomo. He knew some things that matched what I knew. He seemed believable."

"So how come we didn't find any evidence that the warehouse was occupied when we were investigating the attack on Piero Manca?"

"They cleared out after Piero seemed to be onto them. They moved their whole operation, including the girls, into another building, probably the one we targeted for our raid. They seem to have some way to move around without anyone seeing them."

Nic took a sip of soda and added a few more lines to his notes. Robert's account seemed to confirm some of the details the police investigation had uncovered. But one thing didn't make sense. "If you trusted him, why do you think he betrayed you to the thugs running the sex trafficking operation?"

Robert ran his hand through his hair and shook his head. "I can't figure that out," he said. "But he's the only possibility. Otherwise, it would have been someone in our group, and that's hard to believe."

"Has it crossed your mind that he was feeding information about you and your group to the crime ring at the same time he was giving you tips about them?"

"Double-crossing them as well as us?"

Nic nodded.

Robert thought for a moment. "And maybe the ring found out what he was doing. That could explain why he had an 'accident' at the train station, wouldn't it?" He leaned back in his chair, scratching at the stubble on his chin. "There's another possibility, though."

"What is it?"

"That he *had* been providing information to the ring, but for some reason, he stopped. He wasn't useful to them anymore, and he knew too much about them. They had to get rid of him."

There was a long pause before Nic replied. "That's definitely possible."

They ended their conversation with a commitment to meet again if Robert remembered other details about the man in black. They shook hands as Robert looked squarely at Nic. "On that other matter—Julia—you need to know that I intend to fight to keep her."

Nic smiled and nodded. "She is special to both of us,

Robert. We want the best for her. Whatever happens—it's her decision."

After Robert left, Nic retrieved the file in his inbox containing the initial reports on the death at the train station. Spreading it out on his desk, he leafed through it. So far, there wasn't much detail about the investigation, just an account of what had been learned immediately after the accident.

The grisly scene had disrupted travel at the station for several hours. Police needed the time to examine and remove the body and interview some of the bystanders. According to those accounts, the victim had come running down the platform, pushing people out of the way while looking behind him. Was he intending to board an incoming train? No one knew for sure. But as one approached, a man in a blue blazer stepped in his way, and the two collided. The victim was knocked sideways and stumbled for a few steps before he fell onto the tracks just as the train was arriving.

Police assigned to the investigation detained everyone who had witnessed the accident and interrogated them.

Except the man in the blazer. He was nowhere to be found.

CHAPTER 38

The wine bar was packed with tourists and locals enjoying drinks and an early evening snack. It was the kind of place where Robert and Sandro could meet without calling attention to themselves. They would blend right in with the crowd.

Members of their larger group weren't supposed to talk to each other outside meetings—at least not about any activities of the group itself. The cloak of anonymity had to be respected. But the two men, already close friends, now shared an even stronger bond because of the ordeal of the failed raid and the injuries they had suffered as a result of it. So when Robert called Sandro to share what he had learned in his conversation with Nic Rossi, he felt free to mention his new misgivings. "Let's meet after I get off work," Sandro had suggested. "You can tell me what's on your mind."

When Robert arrived, Sandro was already settled at a table at the back of the bar, a glass of Brunello in front of him. Robert ordered his favorite Super Tuscan and a plate of *apperitivi*, which he placed on the table. He pointed at them and motioned to his friend. "Help yourself," he said. He leaned back in his chair and took a deep breath. "It feels good to be out on the town again."

After both had sampled the chips and cheese, Robert leaned forward to look directly at Sandro. "So, how did the meeting go last night?" he asked. Sandro was the only member of their team who had been willing to report to the group about their raid. Giuseppe was still recovering from his injuries, and Antonio, like Robert, had chosen not to attend.

"It was pretty loud and angry," Sandro said.

"That's not typical."

"At least not this bad." Sandro swirled the wine in his glass and sniffed at the bouquet. "I think I liked it better when they focused more on charitable causes—helping the less fortunate and all that. There was less disagreement then."

"A noble enterprise," Robert said. "By the time I joined, their attention was on fighting crime rings and corruption. When did the original mission change?"

"It started as a difference of opinion between young and old members. The young guys felt that more needed to be done to combat violence against women in the community. When you were added, your knowledge of crime in the city sharpened their concerns. That's when they came up with plans to find and expose sex trafficking operations and rescue the girls who were held captive."

"But why did the meeting turn angry when you reported on our raid? We were just following the plans."

"Because it surfaced the old disagreements from the ones who say we're not trained to do this kind of thing. It just convinced them that the efforts to combat crime in Florence should stop. Let the police do the job, they said."

"And ignore the girls who are being victimized—whose lives are being destroyed?"

"Their response to that is that all we're doing is calling attention to ourselves. The syndicates have noticed. Those members of the society claim the attack on our guys in front of the Duomo was a warning to us, a threat of worse things that will happen if we don't back off."

"So, we should give up because we are afraid for our own safety, and not care about vulnerable women and girls?"

"They argue that we should just get back to the work we do best."

"They're all missing the point," Robert said. "We don't have to stop trying to help the victims of the sex trade if we work closely with the police. I think that might be possible. We can provide assistance to the victims once they are rescued—help them into shelters and support them whenever we can."

Sandro nodded. "I agree with you," he said. "But I'm not sure where things will go now. The discussion seemed pretty divided last night."

Both were silent. They sipped their wine and watched the others in the bar who were loudly celebrating the end of the day. Finally, remembering Robert's reason for suggesting they get together to talk, Sandro looked across at his friend. "You said you had some doubts. What are they?"

"It's simple. They need to deal with the person who betrayed our team."

"What do you mean? Wasn't your source of information about the sex trade the guy who tipped off the traffickers?"

"That's what I thought for a while. But now I'm not so sure."

"If it wasn't him, who could it have been?"

Robert took a deep breath. "I've been thinking about it a lot today. I think we were betrayed by another member of our group," he said.

Sandro stared at Robert for several moments before he spoke.

"You can't be serious," he said.

"I am serious. Here's what occurred to me. My source told me about the building where the girls were held. But I never told him exactly when we were going there. The only men who knew about the timing of the raid were those who had attended our meetings. It had to be one of them who tipped off the guards there. Besides, my source seemed genuinely troubled about what was happening to the girls who were being trafficked. I don't know why, but he seemed obsessed with it. He wanted to stop the girls from being harmed."

Sandro frowned. He took a chip from the plate in front of him and bit into it. "You may be right," he said. "But what should we do next?"

"I'm not sure." Robert motioned to the waiter for another glass of wine. "But I know what I'm going to do. I'm quitting the group."

After his long conversation with Sandro, Robert decided to stop by Julia's *pensione*. *If she's there, maybe we can talk. If she isn't ...she might be with Nic.* He had to know. He wasn't going to give up easily in that competition.

Had he drunk too much wine with Sandro? Probably. He bought a bouquet of flowers at an outdoor display. *She loves flowers. This might impress her.*

He stumbled up to the entrance of the *Pensione Europa* and took the elevator up to the registration area. When he asked the desk clerk to ring Julia's room, the man looked curiously at him and smiled. "Our guests are all at dinner," he said. "If those flowers are for her, perhaps you'd like to give them to her in the dining room." He smiled again and pointed down the hall toward the soft sounds of quiet conversation.

Julia was sitting alone at her table, deep in thought as she lingered over a glass of wine. Robert weaved his way over to the table and pulled out the chair opposite her. "May I join you?" he asked. "I've come bearing a gift," he said, waving the bouquet for her to see.

Julia looked surprised, and then laughed, reaching out to accept his present. "You know these aren't necessary," she said. "But I'm going to keep them anyway. They're beautiful."

She motioned to her waiter, pointing at the flowers. "Could you find something for these, please?" He swept them away and returned a few minutes later with them artfully arranged in a classic Tuscan vase, which he placed on the table.

Julia pulled one of the blossoms out of the vase and sniffed it. "And to what do I owe this gesture?" she said, teasing Robert into an embarrassed smile.

"Oh, I don't know," he said, teasing back, "I just found them lying in the street and thought you might like something to brighten up your room."

She laughed. "Seriously. I'm really glad to see you

again," she said and studied his face. "Your bruises seem to be healing."

"Yeah," he said, touching his still-swollen lip. "I saw a doctor. I'm feeling much better than the last time I barged into your life."

They lingered in the dining room long after the other guests had finished dinner. Julia ordered another glass of *pinot grigio* for herself and offered to get a Super Tuscan for Robert. "I'd better have coffee," he answered. "I've probably had enough wine already."

"I probably shouldn't have another glass either," she said, "but this is a special occasion."

"You look sad," he said, looking closely at Julia as the waiter delivered her wine and placed a steaming cup of cappuccino on the table in front of him. "Is everything okay?"

"Nothing I want to talk about now," she answered. "Just thinking about the future." Leaning on her elbows, she swirled the wine in her glass and took a sip. "I'd rather hear what you've been up to since the last time I saw you. You look a lot better than you did then."

Their conversation, lighthearted at first, turned more solemn when he shared with her the details of the raid on the sex trafficking ring.

"I hope you're done with your amateur rescue work after that," she said with concern,

"I think I am," he responded. "I'm definitely done with anything involving the group that organized the raid. But I still would like to know who the turncoat was who tipped off the crooks about our plan. I want him exposed and arrested. I just don't know who can help me find that out."

"Have you told the police?"

"I've talked to Nic, if that's what you mean. But I haven't told him about my suspicions. I want proof before I share that kind of information."

Julia was quiet, thinking about the possibilities Robert could pursue. A couple of ideas came to her. "I think you should tell Nic. Your suspicions may be in line with some of the things he is investigating. And you should tell Carlo. I've been in touch with him a lot lately, and he's been worried about you. He might be able to help you find the answer you're looking for."

"I doubt a poli-sci professor would know that much about the inner workings of the Florentine sex trade," Robert said with a dismissive wave of his hand.

"Maybe not. But he has a colleague—another professor—who is doing research on sex trafficking. He's apparently an expert on the subject. He might know something that addresses your suspicions. Carlo can give you his number at the university. Maybe you can set up a meeting with him."

"Okay. I'll give him a call." He hesitated and cleared his throat. There was much more that he had to say, and he couldn't put it off any longer. "All of this is not really why I came here tonight. I want to talk about us."

"What do you mean?"

"You know what I mean. How serious are you and Nic? Do I have a chance with you?"

Julia looked down, studying her glass of wine, avoiding his eyes. He was one of her oldest and dearest friends. He was one of the reasons she took the assignment to come to Florence. He still meant something to her. But she wasn't sure what.

After a long pause, she looked up at him and said, "I

think that's a conversation that should wait until both of us are sober."

"Are you saying I'm too drunk to think clearly about us?"

"No, Robert," she said in a soft voice. "I think maybe I am."

CHAPTER 39

The waiters in the dining room were clearing away dishes and setting tables for breakfast the next morning. "It's late," Robert said, looking around. "I should be going."

They walked down the corridor away from the dining room, toward the reception area and stopped at the elevator. Robert punched the down button. They stood waiting, listening as the carriage clanked its way upward, moving noisily to their floor. He smiled at Julia, and then leaned forward impulsively, kissing her. Hard. "Ouch!" he cried, pulling back and touching his sore lip.

Both of them laughed. Julia cupped his head in her hands and kissed him on the forehead. "Good night, Robert," she said. "Thank you for tonight. I'm so glad you are safe—and well." She waved at him as the elevator started its descent to the street. Back in her room, she placed the vase of flowers on the coffee table in front of the loveseat. Positioned next to the bouquet Nic had sent her earlier, it added another bright, fresh look to the area.

She rubbed her forehead and sat down, leaning back

against the plump cushions of the overstuffed chair. The pensive mood she had been in when Robert found her in the dining room descended on her again.

I'm getting spoiled. What am I going to do? There are two men in my life, and I can't make up my mind what I want from them.

Her relationship with Nic, intense as it felt, was still new. Was it leading to marriage? He hadn't hinted at that possibility. And she wasn't sure that's what she wanted either. It was too early for that kind of commitment.

What about Robert? Her attraction to him wasn't as deep or as passionate as her feelings about Nic. But they had a long history with each other. "He's a special friend," she said to herself. "Could he be more? Does he want more?"

She stared at the two bouquets and tried to sort out her thoughts. *I wish Amanda was here. She would have some good advice.*

Julia called Carlo the next morning, who put her in touch with Rocco. "I saw Robert last night," she said. "He has some questions that I think maybe you can answer."

Rocco was reluctant at first. "I'll talk to him but only as a favor to you," he said.

When Robert contacted Rocco later in the day, they agreed to meet in his faculty office at the university. It helped that Julia had smoothed the way.

Seated at his desk, Rocco folded his arms, impatient to get the conversation underway. "Julia tells me you're interested in helping victims of sex crimes. So, why do you try to do it through a secret group rather than through other organizations that work with the police?"

Annoyed at first by Rocco's blunt manner, Robert decided to be open with him. "I didn't want just to help the victims after they had been abused. I wanted to belong to a group that focused on completely getting rid of the operations. And I've done enough research on criminal activities that I know sometimes secrecy is crucial."

"Research? What kind of research?"

Robert volunteered the titles of a couple of articles he had written.

"You're the guy who has written those stories about crime in Florence?" Rocco said, friendlier now, and more receptive. "I assign them as readings for students in my seminars on the psychology of crime. They're fantastic."

They had something in common, after all.

Robert relaxed. He wanted to know what Rocco was learning about sex and drug trafficking in Europe. "Is Florence a center of it?" he asked.

"Probably not as much as other cities in Italy or elsewhere in Europe, but that's what I'm trying to find out," Rocco explained. "I'm zeroing in on specific operations here to get an idea of how they are run."

"So, what's your problem with the group I belong to? They're trying to find out some of the same things."

"I don't have a problem with their goal. I admire what they did in the past, helping the poor and the needy. And I respect the desire they have now to rid Florence of the corruption of the criminal syndicates. But men like those in your group are in over their heads trying to oppose the criminals running the rings. This isn't like the rivalries of the past. The Medici could handle the Pazzi. In today's world, well-intentioned, upstanding citizens are no match for the syndicates. It's naive and reckless to think otherwise."

Robert nodded. "I understand. But you must admit some progress is being made on the problem of trafficking. Like the police raid a few days ago. Were you surprised by it?"

"Not really. I knew something was going on. I just wasn't sure where. I didn't expect it to be in that building."

Their conversation was winding down, but Robert had to ask the question that kept nagging at him.

"How do you know so much about my group? Its work is supposed to be secret."

"After I talked to Julia, I checked it out. Some things are pretty obvious. The way your members sometimes sneak around in hooded jackets, for example. And my sources have told me a lot of other stuff."

"Such as?"

"Well, for one thing, they told me that the owner of the building your team tried to raid is a member of your group."

"What?" Robert caught his breath. *So someone in our midst could have betrayed our team.*

Nic hurried to the meeting he had called to give final instructions to the team he had assembled for a special mission. The foursome was already in the room when he arrived and passed out copies of a map he had drawn.

"You'll see here the buildings on the route you'll be following underground. I've been able to figure out their locations after exploring the basements and passages a couple of times on my own."

Luca, the most senior officer in the group, studied his copy of the map and made notations on it as Nic continued his description of their assignment and the reason for it. "If we can shut down a couple of the hidden routes some of the traffickers follow when they're moving from place to place, we may be able to curtail their operations," he said, pointing to routes he suspected after his initial exploration with Renzo. "They depend on secrecy," he added, "and their ability to move out of places before we get to them has always kept them a step ahead of our enforcement efforts. Your mission will be to block access—boarding up entry points wherever you find them."

"Won't we be tampering with vestiges of the past?" Luca asked. He knew that these sites in the historic core of Florence were well protected.

"These passageways may be more recent," Nic explained, "but they're obviously meant to have a function like the connections that used to exist between medieval tower complexes. I doubt that most of the owners of the businesses are even aware of their existence." he added. "They're in places that are either unused or very well concealed from whatever is above ground."

Another member of the team looked concerned. "This sounds like a major project. Aren't we going to need help?"

"I'm guessing that access into underground areas is probably limited to only a few points along the way. We should be able to close down any transit routes pretty quickly."

The team gathered their equipment and, with copies of Nic's map in hand, headed toward the empty warehouse he had marked as the starting point. They would enter the basement and wind their way through the underground labyrinth that Nic had traced on the drawing.

It was over within hours. Nic was sitting outside a

coffee bar, taking a break while he waited for the team to report back to him. Luca and the others saw him as they approached police headquarters. They were covered with dirt, and dots of debris were sprinkled on their worksuits.

"It was more difficult than you predicted," Luca said, sitting down opposite Nic. The other members of the team pulled up chairs at an adjacent table. Luca wiped his brow and continued. "There were several places along the way that we closed. We even checked the side tunnels where the entrances into the passageways led and boarded up those openings, too. No other passages extend as far as the one you and Renzo explored. They stop at basement walls after going through, at most, a couple of buildings."

"But it would still be possible for traffickers to get from one building to another, wouldn't it?"

Luca thought for a moment. "Yes, but they'd be visible once they left the second building they got into."

"Unless they moved the girls into a second building for a while. Maybe taking them out a few at a time from that place."

Luca nodded. "That's possible, yes. Although now we've cut off the underground part of their activities. They'll have to do everything by way of outside routes."

"What about occupants of buildings next to the underground routes? Would they be aware of what was going on?"

"I suppose they could have been. That hotel next to the warehouse, for example. Its tower is pretty close to the alley where an underground passage leads toward other buildings. If anyone downstairs in the hotel was listening when there was activity in the tunnels, they might have heard sounds."

"Outstanding work, men," Nic said. "Now we can

concentrate on following some of the leads we got from our raid the other day. If we're lucky, we might be able to arrest and convict enough of the traffickers that we can drive others away from Florence. Or at least we should be able to rescue more of their victims."

"One more thing, Nic." Luca stood and gathered the equipment he had carried with him. "Some of the underground passages are like the ones Renzo showed you. They're dead ends, like the room where the girls escaped while their apartment was raided. If Renzo and his friend hadn't found them, they wouldn't have been able to get out—not easily. They'd have to go back the way they came, or...."

"Or they'd die there."

"Right."

The possibility of that predicament stopped Nic and the team. No one could speak. Finally, Nic shook his head sadly. "Let's hope we don't find anything like that in any other raids we do."

The next stage of the investigation was aided by the information Rocco provided. His conversation with Robert had persuaded him that some of his evidence was solid enough that it was time to share it with the police.

"There's one thing you should look into," Rocco told Nic. "Some of the captives are not young girls providing service to clients their protectors bring to them. There are a few who have been held as sex slaves for years. If my sources are correct, these women are desperately in need of help. They get traded or sold to other cities or other kinds of sex businesses."

"I'll ask my team to look into that," Nic said.

"Better to coordinate with police teams in other cities. Older women held captive are most likely to have been moved elsewhere."

Nic asked Luca to have someone follow up on Rocco's tip and shifted his own investigation to the man who owned the building the police had raided—a member of Robert's group, Rocco had speculated. "I don't care about that right now," he told Luca. "I just want to know if he is involved with trafficking in other ways than just providing a space for their operations."

The man who owned the building was brought in for questioning. A hulking figure in an expensive suit, he sat down at the table opposite Nic and Luca, folded his arms across his ample midsection, and glowered. He brushed aside their questions about the trafficking operations housed in the building he owned.

"I know nothing of what you found there," he said.

"You weren't aware of what was going on? The comings and goings of men and the girls who were kept there?"

"I just rent space to people who are willing to pay for it," he said. "There's nothing illegal about that."

"Doesn't it concern you that they used the space for sex businesses?"

"I don't know anything about that. But what if they do? Prostitution is legal." He leaned forward and pointed a finger at Nic. "The police in this country haven't done anything to make clear what's illegal and what is not. So what makes you think your investigation will change that?"

He continued to insist that he had done nothing wrong. Finally, he rose and headed toward the door. "I refuse to speak to you any more without my lawyer being present."

After he left, Luca looked at Nic and shrugged. "He's right, you know. This is a crime that isn't taken seriously enough. There aren't the kinds of protections for trafficking victims that there should be."

"I know," Nic said. "But I keep hoping if we uncover the extent of it and make arrests where we can, things will change."

"What should we do about this guy? Should we arrest him?"

"We don't have enough evidence. He'll just continue to claim that he didn't know what was going on."

"But if he tipped off the traffickers about the raid that was planned, he must have known what was in the building."

"We can't prove that either. He'll deny he did it, and the traffickers will, too. The best we can hope for is that he is now scared enough about our being aware of him that he stops providing a base for trafficking operations."

It was time-consuming work. For a few days, Nic wasn't able to see Julia. *I need to get out of here. Take my mind off investigations that aren't going anywhere.* Late in the busy week, he called her. "Let's meet for dinner tonight," he said. "I've missed you."

He was clearing his desk and storing reports in his filing cabinet when one of his fellow inspectors tapped on the door and entered the office. "I just got some new information that I need to share with you." He walked slowly into the room and sat down. He shifted uncomfortably in his chair.

"What's up?" Nic asked, curious about his colleague's awkward behavior. *Something's wrong.*

"Nic, you know I've been assigned to the team investigating Maria's disappearance."

Nic's back stiffened, but he said nothing.

"We haven't had any leads for a long time. The case isn't exactly closed, but...recently I—that is, we—got a tip from one of our other rescues that checked out."

"Have you found her?"

The other man hesitated. "We think so."

"Is she alive?" Nic demanded, leaning forward.

"Yes, but...."

"But what?"

"She's in a hospital. Recovering from drug addiction."

Nic slumped back in his chair. *Oh my God. Maria. My love.* "Can I see her?" he asked, his voice unsteady.

"We can arrange for you to meet the doctor who is treating her. You should hear what she has to say. After that, it'll be her decision about how and when you can see Maria. Be prepared for what the doctor tells you, Nic. Maria may not be ready for a meeting with you."

"Why not?"

"Because her doctor suspects she may have been held hostage somewhere."

Nic clenched his fist. "Tell me who the doctor is," he said. "I want to talk to her as soon as possible. I don't care what Maria's condition is. I want to see her."

I have to see her.

CHAPTER 40

Julia was sitting at their favorite table. Nic was late. It wasn't the first time—police business sometimes came up at the last minute—but this was later than he had ever been. *Maybe he's paying me back. I usually keep him waiting.* Should she leave and go back to her *pensione*? She was beginning to feel a little uncomfortable with the waiter coming by periodically and asking her if she was ready to order.

Just as she was gathering up her purse and preparing to leave, Nic approached the table. She moved over to give him room on the cushion next to her, but he pulled out the chair opposite her at the table and sat down. His eyes were red, and he looked exhausted. *This is bad. Very bad.* He sat quietly, head lowered, and stared at the table in front of him. Finally, he looked up at Julia.

"Julia—I don't know how to say this. Things have changed."

With a trembling voice, he shared with her what he had learned about Maria and her addiction. "I have spoken to her doctor," he said. "She's in pretty bad shape. But I need to be there for her. When she's ready."

Julia said nothing. His pain and grief were obvious. *What about us? Do we have a future together?* The questions that were forming in her mind were selfish, she knew.

After another long silence, Nic continued, "We never talked about where our relationship was leading. You didn't seem to want marriage. I didn't either. I will always be married only to Maria, no matter what," he said.

Julia held her breath. *This is what I have been fearing.*

Nic rubbed his eyes and struggled to find the words he needed to say. "I guess I never gave up hope that she would be found even as I tried to move on," he continued. "And now that she has been found...it's not likely to be the same with her, I know. Unless she gets better...but I still have hope." He paused, unsure of what to say next. "I don't know how much I can do for her. I just know I must be there.... I don't know what that means for you and me."

Julia was crushed. *I love Nic. More than any man since Bill.* Would she be willing to stay in Italy for a relationship so tenuous, so limited as the one he seemed to be hinting at, no matter how strong her feelings were now? *Admit it. It's over.*

She reached across the table and clasped his hand in hers. "You need to concentrate on Maria, however long it takes. I will miss you terribly, but..." Her throat tightened. "But what we have had isn't possible anymore. It's best to end it now."

"I'm sorry, Julia. I didn't mean to hurt you. And I will always care for you. I want you to know that." He kissed her hand, and they sat in silence as the noise of the busy restaurant wrapped around them. Finally, he got up from his chair. "I should go now."

She nodded, unable to speak. He walked slowly away and exited the restaurant. Tears were streaming down her cheeks. She rummaged in her purse and found some Kleenex, dabbing at her eyes as she rose and started toward the entrance.

"Signorina? the waiter called out behind her. She lowered her head and waved him away. Walking even faster, she was out of the restaurant and headed back to the Lungarno before anyone else at the restaurant noticed her departure. By the time she arrived at *Pensione Europa*, she had her feelings under control enough to face dinner. *I'm not hungry, but I should get something to eat.* She got off the elevator and started toward the dining room when she heard Robert's voice behind her, approaching from the reception area where he had been sitting, waiting for her return.

"Julia!" he called out. "Can we talk?"

She swung around to face him. "Not now, Robert!" she shouted. She began to cry again. Robert rushed over and wrapped his arms around her. She buried her head in his shoulder and stood there sobbing. *Hold me. Just hold me tight.*

After several moments, she stepped back and reached for another Kleenex. "Sorry," she said. "Nic and I just broke up. I'm trying to make sense of what happened."

He wiped the tears from her cheeks.

"I don't want to be alone tonight, Robert."

"Let me take you back to my place. I'll fix dinner."

"No expectations. I just need company."

"Of course," he said. "No expectations."

He waited in the reception area as she went to her room and returned with an overnight bag. "Let's go. I have to get out of here."

And they were on their way.

After dinner in Robert's apartment, Julia sat with her legs curled up under her on the couch which took up much of the space in the cramped living room. Robert reclined in the lounge chair that he pulled from the area next to the fireplace so he could be closer to her. Plates with remnants of the quick meal of pasta and insalata he had prepared for them were on the coffee table between them.

Julia held a glass of Chianti, sipping the wine slowly while she described her painful conversation with Nic at Paoli and his distress about Maria's horrifying fate. "I understand why he needs to be with her," she said. "It's the right thing to do. But the end of our relationship happened so fast, I don't know what to do next." Her tears had stopped now. She was focusing more on what steps to take personally and professionally, trying to figure out a plan for the next part of her stay in Florence.

"I can't continue to stay in the *pensione*," she said. "As reasonable as its rates are, I won't be able to afford living there much longer."

"Why not? I thought the magazine took care of that."

"Robert, I'm no longer on their expense account. That didn't cover everything, but it paid enough to help me get by. The rent money from my house covered my other costs. I just always assumed I would nail down some other freelancing assignments to help me pay for the rest of my year in Italy."

"Are you sure the magazine has accepted your essay? And you'll be paid?"

"Yes, they've told me they're going to run the piece in

an issue a couple of months from now. They'll wire the payment."

"When did you hear from them?"

"I got their final decision yesterday. I was going to share the news with Nic at dinner tonight so we could celebrate...Ironic, isn't it? I was going to take him up on his offer of moving in with him."

She was going to move in with him? They were that serious? Robert was disappointed but didn't want to show it. He rose from his chair and picked up their dinner plates, taking them into the kitchen. He returned in a few minutes with a plate of cheese and sourdough bread.

"What are you going to do now?" he asked as he put the food on the coffee table.

"I had already pitched a couple of ideas to the magazine for other assignments about travel in Tuscany so I could stay in Florence." She shook her head as if to throw off all that had changed so abruptly. "They might still come through. If they do…I guess I'll stick around here for a while."

Any further discussion of Nic was unlikely for a while. Julia was concentrating on other problems. And Robert wanted to focus on what the two of them could do together.

"You're always welcome to stay here. I'm no longer going to be involved in tracking down sex traffickers," he said with a smirk. "I'll have time to show you some parts of Florence and Tuscany that are special to me."

"Well thank heavens you're done with your risky pastime." She paused, her look turning serious. "But I don't think I'm ready to stay here. I need to be by myself for a while. Maybe later."

Maybe later? There's still hope!

CHAPTER 41

They talked until it was well past midnight. By then, both were exhausted. "You have to stay somewhere tonight," he said, stretching. "It might as well be here." Yawning, she agreed.

She slept on the sofa bed in Robert's office and got up late. A note was attached to his refrigerator door: *"Gone shopping. There's a little food in the cupboards. OJ in the fridge. Help yourself."*

After pouring herself a cup of the coffee he had brewed, she carried it along with a plate of fruit and a croissant to the small dining room table. She was finishing her breakfast when he returned with a couple of bags of groceries.

"I figured I needed a better supply of food if I'm going to have a house guest," he said as he put things away.

"That'll do for our meals, Robert, but I really do have to find a place where I can be on my own."

A call to Carlo led to another option once she explained the changes she needed to make in her circumstances. "At this time of year, an extended day room might be available at the Student Hotel," Carlo suggested.

She and Robert checked it out that afternoon and arranged for her to move in the next day. When she called to thank Carlo for his recommendation, he had even more good news. "I asked around and found that there's an office at the university that is looking for a short-term graphic designer to help them with a couple of publications they're preparing for the millennium. It won't be a lot of money, but it will help until you find a more permanent position—if that's what you want."

That night, over another pasta dinner, Robert talked more about what was ahead. "I'll help you move out of the *Europa*. And I'll ask some of my business contacts about other possibilities for you. This is such a busy tourist season, there may be some part-time jobs open."

The next morning, they drove to the *pensione,* and Robert waited in the reception area as she packed her bags. The desk clerk was surprised at her sudden departure. "Were there problems with your stay here, *signorina*?" he asked as he handed her the receipt for her lodging.

"Oh no," she said quickly. "I loved it here. And I'll be back, in the future. Something just came up."

The clerk smiled and looked at Robert. "I understand. We will look forward to seeing you again, then."

He thinks she has something going on with me. I should be so lucky.

Once Julia had moved into her accommodation at the Student Hotel, she and Robert returned to his apartment. "The room is okay," she told him, "but it's not the kind of place where you can spend a lot of time. It's just for sleeping."

"That's fine with me," Robert said. "I like your

company. And besides," he said smiling, "I need someone to help me eat all that food I bought yesterday."

Julia laughed despite the sadness that she was feeling about the sudden disruption in her life. "Good! I think you may be stuck with me for a while."

"But tonight, we should celebrate. Let me take you to dinner."

"Not at Paoli, please."

"No, nothing that touristy. I've discovered a place that I think you'll enjoy. Quiet, known only to locals, great food. And they'll let us linger as long as we want to over dinner."

"Sounds perfect!"

It was a trattoria tucked away in a piazza near Robert's apartment, modest in decor but clearly popular with a neighborhood clientele. No tourists. They settled at the only available table at the back of the room, near the kitchen. Robert ordered glasses of Chianti and house specials for them. "It's a single item menu," he explained. "The selection changes every night, but it's always good."

As they waited for the first course, Julia was curious about how Robert supported himself in Florence. "I know you've told me some of this before but how do you make enough money to live here?"

"A lot came from the inheritance I got when Dad died. I invested it and the dividends are pretty good. And I get royalties from my novel about the Medici era. If you can believe it, that sold well in local bookstores. Plus, I have magazines that are always interested in the research pieces I write about crime in Italy."

"You've also told me that you teach occasionally."

"Right."

"Where?"

"In classes offered by American universities who bring tour groups in the summer to Florence."

"Is that how you know Amanda?"

"Yes. I met her as part of my work with those tours. She was very successful as a guide."

"Do you think I might have a chance at that kind of teaching? I could use more stable income than I'll earn in the temporary position Carlo has lined up, even if my freelance assignments pan out."

"Not now, probably. Those arrangements are made well in advance of the tourist season."

Julia was discouraged, but she wanted to know more about his way of life. What motivated him. "Your crime stories…they're so different from other things you have written. How did you get into that line of work?"

"Long story. It started when it occurred to me that the criminal intrigue I was describing in the days of the Medici might have a modern counterpart. So I started watching local news coverage carefully to see what crimes were being reported regularly. I followed that up with some research in the library. And then I contacted the police to see if there were trials and investigations they could tell me about. That's how I met Nic. He was my contact for that information. The crimes that shocked me most involved trafficking of all kinds—drugs, human trafficking, sex trafficking. There's so much of it going on. Not just here but worldwide. I admit I became angry and somewhat obsessive about trying to expose the wrongdoing I was discovering. I wanted to do something more than just write about it."

"You always did go full throttle on any social problems you cared about," Julia said. "Is that how you got involved with the group you've been part of?"

"Yes, I was describing what I had found out to a guy named Sandro—a friend of mine from university activities I was involved in. He introduced me to the group."

"Why do you use a pseudonym for those articles?"

"Safety. I didn't want the crime rings to know I was on to them. If they know who I am, they might come after me."

Tearing off a piece of bread from the loaf the waiter had brought to their table, Robert looked around the trattoria before he added in a quiet voice, "I have an idea that might be an interesting possibility for both of us, if you're willing. It's something I've already pitched to a magazine. A big project," he explained. "An in-depth study. If you're interested, we can do it together."

Robert described the positive response he had received from his contact. "He was interested in the angle I proposed. The contradiction of sex trafficking going on at the same time the religious Jubilee is bringing pilgrims to Italy. He liked the focus I had in mind—the human side—the victims, their circumstances, and how they suffer."

"That sounds like something I would like to do," Julia said.

They spent the rest of the evening over dinner and then back at his apartment, making lists of possible sources and deciding which ones each of them would interview. Julia agreed to reach out to Rocco and Renzo. Robert would talk to Sandro and Giuseppe, both of whom had seen the impact of sex trafficking on the young women who were victimized. And he would get back in touch with sources he had relied on for his other articles on crime in the city.

"How about Nic?" he asked as they were dividing up their assignments. "He was my original source for a lot of the things I learned about trafficking in Tuscany."

"You should contact him. He knows what you've already discovered," Julia said, avoiding eye contact with Robert, concentrating on the notes she was taking on their plans. "And besides, he may welcome the chance to think about something other than Maria's condition."

Great! She doesn't want to see him. There may still be hope.

CHAPTER 42

Julia's first interview was with Renzo, who arranged a visit for her at the shelter where he had taken the two girls he and Amanda had encountered in the underground room. The women running the shelter were reluctant to talk about specific victims, but they were eager to show Julia their facility and talk in general about girls they had helped. "This is a problem that no one takes seriously enough," one of them told her. "The police, government officials—nobody. I'm glad you are going to shed some light on what is going on."

Later in the week, over coffee at the *pasticceria* where they had met before, Rocco provided Julia with other references she could tap and shared insights from his own investigations. "A little advice. If I were you," he told her, "I'd use pseudonyms rather than your own names on this. You never know how the crime rings are going to react if their work is exposed. You might become a target."

Julia nodded. "Robert's already aware of that. We'll be careful."

Sandro and Giuseppe were glad to share what they had

found out about trafficking after their failed raid. "The more people know about what is going on, the more progress might be possible." They referred Robert to other members of the group who were concerned about the prevalence of the sex trade in Italy.

Julia and Robert met every evening to discuss what they learned. She provided Robert with copies of several photographs she had taken but not used in her travel essay—scenes she had captured of sex workers lingering on the streets. I like these," Robert said. "They give a human face to the problem."

Over a period of weeks, as spring turned to summer, they put the manuscript together, fitting their work around the graphic design project that took up Julia's time during the day.

When he had finished a rough draft of the series, Robert sent a copy to Rocco, who had expressed interest in seeing it. He was back in touch quickly. "This is very good," he said. "A powerful indictment of the communities that do nothing about this crime." He suggested a few changes, mainly about the location of trafficking operations. "Be careful with giving out information that may not have been confirmed yet," he warned. "If it's incorrect, the owners of those sites will charge you with falsely incriminating them. And even if it's correct, it may still be part of an ongoing, confidential investigation by the police. Don't get in their way."

"Should we show this to Nic?" Julia asked Robert that evening as they were revising the piece.

Robert was quiet. He shuffled the pages they had been reviewing, set them aside and looked at Julia. "I didn't tell you this before because I didn't want to alarm you. I tried to reach him, but no one could tell me where to find him. He has apparently gone missing."

Journal

I don't know where to start. The worst thing I could imagine has happened and there's not a thing I can do about it. Nic is missing. Apparently, the police are worried because it was so sudden. Robert told me about it last night. He did his best to reassure me, but I had to come back to my room in the Student Hotel. To be alone. I've spent the rest of the night going over everything I've been dealing with. Remembering what Nic and I did together.

.He was already out of my life. A few weeks now. I still miss him, but the pain of losing him has been easing a bit. He called me a couple of days ago. Told me he hasn't seen Maria yet. She is slowly making progress. He says he has taken a leave of absence from work so he can be with her when her doctor tells him it is possible. He seemed to be in good spirits. There was no clue that he was about to disappear.

I moved out of the Europa. Didn't want to stay there any longer. The magazine liked my photo essay and it's scheduled to appear in an upcoming issue. But they're not covering my expenses anymore. And there were too many memories of Nic there.

Robert has been great. I have dinner with him every night, usually at his apartment. He's not pushing a romantic relationship. That's good. I'm not ready for that right now. But I enjoy his company. He's sweet, smart, and fun to be around. But all I can think of now is Nic. Where is he? Is he safe?

CHAPTER 43

Luca had called Robert to inquire about Julia's whereabouts. He wanted to see her immediately. At the police station.

Robert insisted on accompanying her. "If Nic's disappearance is related in any way to the sex trafficking investigations he was working on, we might have some information from our research that could be helpful." At least, that was the way he explained his reason for going with her. Mainly, he was worried about her state of mind. She obviously hadn't slept much, and she seemed agitated and fragile. She needed strength and support. That's what he could provide.

"Have you and Nic been together recently?" Luca asked. He was sitting behind the desk in Nic's office when Robert and Julia arrived. His manner was blunt, to the point. This was no time to dodge the obvious issue. He knew that Nic and Julia had been having an affair.

"Not for weeks," she said, her voice thin, almost inaudible. Shaky. "We broke up when he found out about Maria...." She paused and tried to compose herself. "He called me recently, but that's the only time I've heard from him."

"What did you talk about?"

"Maria, mainly. How she was doing. What her doctor had told him."

"Did he sound upset? Angry?"

"No, not at all. He just sounded...hopeful."

Luca leaned back in his chair and searched her face. "Did he hint at going anywhere? Or doing anything other than visit Maria?"

"No. What do you mean?"

Robert interrupted. He could tell she was confused by Luca's line of questioning. "Officer, where's this heading? What's this all about? When you called me yesterday, you told me that Nic had gone missing. But obviously, Julia doesn't know where he is."

Luca nodded and put down the pen he was using to take notes on their conversation. "I know," he said, his tone betraying the weariness and anxiety he was feeling. "I'm just hoping to get some hint, some tiny detail that might add up to enough to lead us to where he is."

"What do you have so far?" Robert persisted.

"Only that we know Nic was aware that Maria had been held as a sex slave."

"What? Who told him?"

Luca didn't answer for a moment. "I'm afraid I did. I was giving him an update on the trafficking investigation he had been part of. I thought if he knew what had been done to Maria, he would help us track down who had kept her. But he was furious. Stormed out of the office. And we haven't been able to find out where he went."

"Did he know enough about your investigation that he would go after those who had held her captive?"

"Probably. That's what I'm afraid of."

The next week, Robert spent as much time as he could with Julia, trying to distract her from her obvious distress about Nic's disappearance. She completed her work on the graphic design project at the university, and Robert put finishing touches on their article and sent it to the magazine for review. Most of their hours together were spent on activities that would remind her more of why she had returned to Florence in the first place. Renewing her love for the city and its attractions. Sightseeing. Eating out, enjoying drinks at his favorite wine bar. Spending evenings together at his apartment, often over dinner, sometimes simply enjoying quiet times without conversation. Reading. They even took a couple of day trips, driving in his Fiat to Siena and Pisa.

And they talked a lot. About Florence. About the fact that neither of them had settled into a conventional career. About their memories of their student days.

As their work and their time together expanded, dinner had become a joint project. Robert confessed that he was running out of recipes beyond the pasta repertoire that was his specialty.

"Let me take over," she said. "I've missed cooking. And I admit I got tired of hotel meals and eating out." They divided cooking chores, with Julia preparing the entrees and salads, drawing on her memory of favorites from an Italian cookbook her mother had given her, and Robert concentrating on desserts and wine selection.

One night, lingering over gelato and biscotti, Julia raised her glass of wine and smiled at Robert. "We make a good team," she said. Robert touched his glass to hers. "To us," he replied.

"So, does your offer of having me as a house guest still stand?"

Robert had just taken a bite of pasta when she spoke. *Is she serious?* He coughed and finished swallowing before he could answer. "Of course! Are you interested?"

"Totally," she said. "I've been thinking. I don't spend much time at the Student Hotel. I'm mainly here. It's a waste of money for me and someone else can probably make better use of that space."

"We can check you out of there as soon as you want. I'll move some things around here so you can settle in." He was trying not to show his excitement at the prospect of having her stay with him. *Maybe she wants to be something more than a guest. I'll get the bedroom ready.*

"Thanks, Robert. No need for big changes." Their relationship wouldn't be different. She had to make that clear. "The sofa bed is still fine with me."

Damn!

CHAPTER 44

Conversations had become even more comfortable between them. They continued to talk about everything. But never about Nic, until one night when they were cooking dinner together, as she was cutting up to vegetables and greens, she asked casually, "If the police continue to say Nic is missing, does that mean they actually think he is dead?"

"Not necessarily," Robert said, surprised that the question seemed to come out of nowhere. Had it been on her mind since their meeting with Luca at the police station? "He may have voluntarily gone into hiding."

She nodded and scooped the salad fixings into a bowl. She never brought up the topic again.

The pattern of their lives had taken on an easy familiarity. *Sort of like being a married couple, but without the sex. I wish there was more. But does she?*

She surprised him after a few more weeks of the routine that had taken over their relationship. During an evening of reading and quiet conversation, she rose from the couch that was her favorite place to relax and took his hand, pulling him to his feet and leading him into his bedroom. They made love, tentatively at first, and then with the same passion they had for each other when they were in college. Wrapped in each other's arms afterward, Robert asked, "So what just changed?"

"Nothing has changed, Robert. I just needed to feel close to someone again."

Another pattern emerged after that. Sometimes, she was distant, interested only in dinner conversations and reading. But occasionally, she welcomed his invitation to join him in bed. Their lovemaking was ardent and uninhibited. She wasn't faking it, he could tell. She was actually enjoying it. And then she would put a distance between them again, spending days by herself, sightseeing alone, resisting his attempts at playful banter over dinner.

I have to be patient. She's obviously trying to work through a lot. But this is hard.

Later, she surprised him again, this time over breakfast.

"I've decided to go to some of the other places that I had intended to visit this year before I became so involved with things in Florence. And I have some ideas for other stories I can do."

"That's great," he said. "Another article about Florence?"

"No. Other places in Tuscany. And after that, I'll be based in Rome."

"Rome? Why?" He tried to hide his disappointment.

"For the Jubilee. I got a letter from the magazine that published my article about the millennium. They liked it enough that now they're going to set me up with an apartment in Rome so I can cover some of the opening events of the Jubilee. It'll be a feature on people traveling there as pilgrims. Not a story on the religious aspect of the year.

I'm not qualified to do that. I'll focus on the travel angle—why people choose to go on a pilgrimage. The activities that interest them."

"So you'll be leaving Florence?" He knew how selfish he sounded, but suddenly he was absorbing the reality of the fact that she was leaving him, too.

She noticed. "Robert, I'm sorry. I never planned to spend the whole year In Florence. It was always going to be a very expensive part of my tour of Italy. I've saved enough now that I can go see some other sites."

"While you're focusing on Tuscany, we can go together on some more day trips."

"No. I have to get out of here. Alone. You've been wonderful, but I haven't been able to get the thing with Nic out of my mind. I need to be someplace other than Florence. I'll be preoccupied enough with travel and working on possible stories that maybe I can put this other stuff behind me."

They talked more about the assignment in Rome over dinner, and Robert did his best to appear happy for her. "Can I come visit you there?" he asked, trying to sound playful but hoping she would agree.

She laughed. "Maybe after a while," she said. "I'll probably be pretty busy." She stopped. Robert was clearly crestfallen. "Sure. That would be fun. But later, okay?"

"At least I can help you move, right? And after that, we can stay in touch by phone."

"It's a deal," she said.

CHAPTER 45

Nic had been away for too long. He contacted Maria's doctor as soon as he had been told about her condition, but after that he simply stayed in touch while he completed his own secret mission. The doctor had advised him that Maria needed to be given time to heal before she could reunite with him.

So this was his first visit to the hospital, a shaded and sequestered facility known for its rehabilitation of people suffering from serious problems of drug addiction. Today, he would be meeting in person with Dr. Russo, who promised a more complete diagnosis and an update on Maria's progress.

Dr. Russo, tall, thin, and unsmiling, with her graying blonde hair pulled back into a tight bun, met him in her office. "I'm pleased we can finally meet, Mr. Rossi," she said as they shook hands. "Let's begin with a walk through the hospital grounds," she added, inviting him to follow her out of the hospital building into the tree-lined garden area outside. "I want you to see the surroundings for Maria's treatment. It's meant to create a calming, comfortable environment for patient recovery."

Dr. Russo talked as the two of them strolled along the paths that wound through the garden. "I know you have wanted to know more of the details of what happened to Maria. The police are sure she was kidnapped. By a sex trafficking ring. From that point on, it's not clear what was done to her, but it's typical of the traffickers to beat, rape, and drug those they have captured. She has injuries consistent with that kind of abuse."

O dio. My precious Maria.

"Her physical injuries have been treated, of course. But our purpose in this facility has been first to help her recover from her addiction and then treat the mental trauma she experienced in her captivity."

Nic couldn't understand. It wasn't like Maria to have submitted to that kind of abuse. She had always been so strong, so independent. "Why didn't she resist or try to escape?"

"She may have. But the physical abuse would have been worse if she had. And those who held her captive would have kept her drugged. Her addiction was very strong by the time we brought her here. She had to be helped with withdrawal from the drugs she had come to depend on."

"I've visited with some victims of trafficking—in the shelters after they were rescued. Most of them were young and frightened, but they didn't seem to be traumatized."

"Had they been held captive for long? If they were, I doubt they were entirely free of mental health complications." A hint of impatience was in Dr. Russo's voice. She was clearly intolerant of Nic's assumption that the young women he had seen hadn't suffered emotional difficulties.

She stopped at a bench on the edge of the garden and turned to look directly at Nic. "Victims of sex trafficking—especially older and long-term victims like Maria—have been through a trauma that leaves them suffering from something very much like PTSD. They need extensive counseling to deal with that."

Nic sat down on the bench and lowered his head, eyes closed. He had to compose himself, get his emotions under control. *This is worse than I ever imagined.*

He sat up straight and pulled his shoulders back. "Is there anything I can do to help her?"

"Not right now. I don't think we're there yet."

"Why not?" Desperation was creeping into his voice.

Dr. Russo spoke again, calmly. "Because it's the nature of the trauma she has suffered. She doesn't trust anyone—certainly not anyone she hasn't been with lately. She has become as dependent on her captors emotionally as she is physically on the drugs they were giving her."

It sounds hopeless.

"Would you like to see her, Mr. Rossi?"

"Yes! Is that possible?"

"I think she might be ready for that, at least. Follow me."

Nic and Dr. Russo walked back through the garden into the hospital, heading down a corridor that led to another wing of the building. He was struggling to control his excitement, wanting the doctor to move faster. She took her time until they stopped at the entrance to a room halfway down the hall. She turned to him, her hand poised above the door handle. "Don't get your hopes up, Mr. Rossi," she cautioned. "Take things slowly."

She opened the door onto a large area that appeared to be a break room of some sort. Tables and chairs were arranged in clusters. Maria sat in a chair close to the wall opposite the entrance, next to a window. She was gazing at the scenery outside.

She's so thin. And she doesn't look well. Will she recognize me?

Nic hesitated for a moment before he felt the doctor's hand on his back, pushing him forward. He walked slowly toward Maria, stopping a few feet away from where she sat.

"Maria?" he said, his voice trembling.

She turned toward him. Her gaze seemed vacant and lifeless. For a moment, she appeared to be confused. And then she reached out her hand.

"Nic?"

CHAPTER 46

"On the Road in Tuscany" was the title Julia had in mind for her first article. She rented a car and made a leisurely journey from Siena during the Palio to Lucca, Pisa and Chianti country in late summer. When she felt she had enough photos and impressions for that article, she returned to Florence to meet up with Robert for their drive to Rome. By then, it was early fall, and she was eager to do more research on the Jubilee, helped by several sources of information he had found for her.

Once in Rome, he presented her with a winter coat—an early Christmas present, he said. "The wardrobe you brought with you for spring in Florence is pretty adaptable to autumn here, but you'll need something really warm in December."

"Robert, that is so sweet of you!" She wrapped her arms around his waist and kissed him. They made love again that night. He left the next morning for Florence, and she turned her full attention to the writing assignment that had brought her to the Holy City.

The Great Jubilee as envisioned and decreed by Pope John Paul II, she remembered from her conversations with Robert, was to be a period of penitence and ecumenical celebration. Debt relief for the poorest nations was a theme the Pope wanted to receive particular prominence. Other journalists she encountered while exploring the city were focusing their attention on religion and politics. Her approach would be more personal.

"I'm planning to attend the major events at the beginning of the Jubilee year," she told Robert during one of their phone calls. "The opening of the holy doors at St. Peter's on Christmas Eve and then at other churches after the beginning of the year. I'll interview pilgrims I run into there. I want to know what the Jubilee means to them."

The first few months of the new millennium were filled with other celebrations. She would go to as many as she could as she put the article together. The magazine wanted to run it before the closing of the Jubilee in January of 2001.

Her life took on a discipline that became routine for her. Time passed quickly, compressed by the monotonous rhythm of her work and the absence of a social life, and hastened by her awareness that her year in Italy was coming to an end. She didn't socialize much with the other journalists she ran into, but she didn't want to. She had little in common with them. Her only friends were a group of middle-aged tourists she met while doing interviews for her article. They invited her to dinner at a restaurant near their hotel several times. She enjoyed the diversion and the company. They were intrigued by the writing assignments she had taken on and the amount of time she was spending in Italy.

"What did you do after you finished the article about

the millennium in Florence?" Alma asked. One of the older women in the group. This was not her first trip to Italy.

"I hung around hoping to hear if some of the other assignments I pitched to editors had come through."

"Wasn't that rather expensive? Florence hotels are pricey in high season."

"Oh, I wasn't in a hotel the whole time. I was staying with a guy I knew."

Alma beamed. She had stumbled on a juicy tidbit about Julia's love life. "Staying with a guy? A boyfriend?"

"Not a boyfriend. Just a friend."

Except you don't sleep so often with someone who is just a friend.

Robert came to see her in Rome on weekends when he was able to get away from his writing and teaching responsibilities. On the first visit, he brought the issue of the magazine featuring their long piece on sex trafficking. "It has already had an impact," he said. "Local authorities in Florence seem to be taking to heart our calls for greater attention to the problem. And Sandro tells me our group has begun to focus its work on the victims of trafficking. Oh, by the way, the warehouse next to the *Torrevecchia* — it's for sale again. The mysterious owner has apparently left town."

During another visit, over dinner at a trattoria in the neighborhood of her apartment, he brought other news. "Nic has returned to the police department with lots of information he uncovered about one of the rings running the sex trade. There have apparently been several key arrests."

"That's fantastic!" she said. "But why haven't I read anything about it in the papers here in Rome?"

"Probably because it's more of a local success. Trafficking is still a problem throughout the rest of Italy and Europe. And the police are protecting Nic. Luca told me that he had gone underground, working with sources Rocco had suggested. If the police or the news revealed too much about where the information came from, Nic and Rocco might be targeted."

"What about Maria? Is she out of the hospital?"

"Not yet, but she's better now. Nic has been able to see her quite often. Her doctor decided she could handle it. They're not back together, but it's looking like more of a possibility."

Julia felt a twinge of jealousy, and she tried to put it out of her mind. *I should be happy for them,* she thought. "Nic said he wanted to bring to justice those who abducted Maria," she said to Robert. "Looks like he has done it."

After dinner, they strolled through the Piazza Navona and the streets surrounding the Pantheon, checking out the bustling nightlife. "This kind of scene just isn't my thing anymore," he said. "Am I getting old?"

Julia couldn't resist teasing him. "Robert, this kind of scene has never been your thing!" They both laughed.

Robert stayed overnight in her apartment and left the next day for Florence. She was alone again, facing another round of visits and interviews and finally settling down to writing. Her work on the article wound down as the year's series of celebrations proceeded. The Pope still had a pilgrimage to Israel scheduled, and there was the closing ceremony early in the new year, but most of the other activities were quite similar, and the reflections shared by the tourists she talked to weren't adding anything to those she had already heard. She decided she had captured the spirit and the meaning of the pilgrimage for the church and those who had made the trip to Rome. She assumed it was the same with the celebrations taking place elsewhere in the world. The Great Jubilee was as ecumenical and global as the Pope had intended. And the debt relief message was gaining traction in a movement that attracted international press coverage.

Her time now was spent in more personal pursuits. Enjoying dinner out on her own and with friends she met doing interviews and attending Jubilee activities in the city. Taking long walks around the city when the weather permitted. She even attended services at a couple of the pilgrimage churches. Sightseeing.

There was enough free time for her to venture to other locations she had always wanted to explore. She bought a rail pass and made several short trips to Southern Italy, a region she had never visited before. She signed up for expeditions to Herculaneum and Pompeii, Capri and the Amalfi Coast.

While on a trip to Naples, lingering over a midday meal, she eavesdropped on vacationers sitting near her at a restaurant on the waterfront near the Castel dell'Ovo. They were discussing news stories they had heard about crime in the city. "I read that sex trafficking is rampant here. Why doesn't someone do something about it?" She smiled. *If Robert were here, he'd probably start up a conversation with that guy.*

Robert. On her mind again.

But despite all her excursions and her opportunity to live in one of the most fascinating cities in the world, something was missing. Her love of Italy and her desire to experience it fully now seemed empty.

March approached. The anniversary of her return to the country of her birth. She decided to celebrate quietly by cooking dinner for herself. Seated at the small table in the corner of her apartment kitchen, lingering over a glass of *pinot grigio*, she struggled to sort out her feelings. *I've done all the traveling I wanted to do and did some good work along the way. What's next? I'm a year older and not any happier. And I have no clue about how to find whatever it was that I came here looking for.*

She gathered up her dinner plate and silverware, depositing them in the kitchen sink and then carried her glass of wine into the small living room. She settled on the couch, placed her glass on the table in front of her, and gazed out the window that overlooked the piazza below, with a view of the city beyond. The sky was brilliant with color. Sunset on another beautiful spring day.

What's wrong? What's missing?

The doorbell rang. She got up, walked over to the entryway, and opened the front door. Robert stood there grinning, holding a huge bouquet of flowers and a bottle of Chianti. "I was in the neighborhood and thought I'd stop by to say hello."

Stifling a giggle, she smiled at him and accepted the flowers. He followed her into the living room, carrying the wine and a suitcase. Standing close to her, he watched as she arranged the bouquet in a vase that she placed on the coffee table.

"If it's okay with you," he said after she was done, "I plan to be here for a while."

She turned around, wrapped her arms around his neck, and kissed him.

"Stay as long as you want. I've missed you."

CHAPTER 47

Julia woke to the sound of church bells.
She raised her head from her pillow, rubbed her eyes, and looked around.

Robert emerged from their bathroom in the *Hotel Torrevecchia*, toweling down after a shower. After a few days of sightseeing in Rome, he had convinced her to return with him to Florence. "You can polish your Tuscany and Rome pieces there. I'll help if you want."

He walked over to the bed and lay next to her, leaning over to kiss her.

"I see why you like this hotel so much."

"It's a good place for beginning a new adventure."

"A new adventure? Like what?" He smiled and kissed her again.

"Well, for me, at first, it was a new way of life. But now it's coming to terms with everything that has happened since the last time I stayed here. It has been an incredible year. I have learned so much about Florence."

"What surprised you the most?"

She sat up, arranged a couple of pillows against the

headboard of the bed, and leaned against them. "The way the past and the present really do coexist. I know we've talked about that before, but I didn't realize the extent of it. It's embedded in the way people think. The explanations they have for what happens. The Medici, or modern versions of them, still fight with their rivals. Beauty still flourishes despite the presence of corruption. And the goodness of Florence always prevails."

"That sounds like the opening lines of another magazine piece."

She laughed. "Maybe. I've given it a lot of thought. Especially when I was in Rome, surrounded by all those ceremonies of repentance."

"I think it's a great idea for an article. We can make this the first one we work on as a married couple."

She nodded absentmindedly, lost in thought about the possibilities. Both of them were quiet for a few moments. Suddenly, she sat up and looked over at Robert. "Did you just propose marriage?"

He laughed and reached out to pull her close. She cupped his face in her hands and kissed him.

"I thought you'd never ask."

EPILOGUE

JOURNAL

We were married at the end of June in a small ceremony at a villa in the Tuscan countryside. I know it's corny, but I've always dreamed of having a summer wedding. The photos turned out great. Robert still has the beard he grew while his face was healing from the wounds he had suffered in the raid. He thinks it makes him look more distinguished. I told him I think it makes him look rugged and sexy. He just laughed. His friends Sandro, Giuseppe and Antonio attended. Carlo came with his partner. Rocco was by himself. Mom flew in from Seattle with my stepdad. She was thrilled to see Florence again, after having left under such sad circumstances earlier in her life. We made sure the two of them were able to stay at the Torrevecchia while they were here. She loved it. She said she met Piero, the bartender. Apparently, he still remembers me. Amanda sent a gift—a reservation for a weekend in one of the places in the Cinqueterra where she has connections. Renzo presented it to us with a flourish. Amanda also included a note promising to visit us when she returns for *her annual stay. Even Nic came, although not for long. Maria is still not fully recovered.*

Robert and I have moved to a larger apartment in his building. My articles on Tuscany and on the Jubilee in Rome have been submitted and are under review. And we are trying to decide how to move ahead with the piece on the connections between past and present in Florence.

Why were there so many twists and turns to get to this point? So much was beyond our control. Maybe that's why. That's the lesson. Every change in life takes its own path, at its own pace. You have to be prepared for whatever comes your way.

I love you, Robert. I know now how long and how deeply you have loved me. I'm so happy you waited for me to understand and treasure that. And my beautiful Florence—you have become as much a part of me as I am a part of you. The story I hold clasped in my heart now dwells in yours.

I'm ready for my next chapter.

ABOUT THE AUTHOR

Jerilyn McIntyre is a communication professor and university administrator emerita, history scholar, and an author whose work has appeared in a variety of professional and literary journals.

She has published in several genres, from academic research to personal essays, short fiction, and a few humorous stories chronicling the adventures of Harley, a charismatic black cat. All of these were aimed at adult readers. She has also published three novellas for middle-grade readers—Paws in the Piazza, The Shadow of the Unscratchable, and Enchanted: Time and the Mountain

ALSO BY JERILYN MCINTYRE

Middle Grade Fiction:

Paws in the Piazza

Passi Felpati e Felini Alati (With Grazia Adami Lovi)

The Shadow of the Unscratchable Enchanted: Time and the Mountain

Humorous Short Stories:

Furball: A Harley T. Katt Adventure Harley Finds His Voice

Paws at Odds

Personal Essays and Memoirs:

Death in Florence Beginnings Epiphany

Foiling Gravity

Loo in the Time of Coronavirus Passages

To Remember Them as They Lived Lincoln School Redux

www.ingramcontent.com/pod-product-compliance
Lightning Source LLC
Chambersburg PA
CBHW071157140325
23506CB00013B/959